CW00508288

EMMA FROST MYSTERY - BOOK 7

EASY AS ONE TWO THREE

WILLOW ROSE

A, B, C!
It's easy as
One, two, three,
as simple as
Do, re, mi,
A, B, C,
one, two, three!
Baby you and me girl!

FROM THE SONG ABC BY THE JACKSON FIVE
WRITTEN BY JEFFERSON, QUINCY/KARAN, OLIVE

BOOKS BY THE AUTHOR

HARRY HUNTER MYSTERY SERIES

- All The Good Girls
- Run Girl Run
- No Other Way
- Never Walk Alone

MARY MILLS MYSTERY SERIES

- What Hurts the Most
- You Can Run
- You Can't Hide
- Careful Little Eyes

EVA RAE THOMAS MYSTERY SERIES

- Don't Lie to me
- What you did
- Never Ever
- Say You Love me
- Let Me Go
- It's Not Over
- To Die For

EMMA FROST SERIES

- Itsy Bitsy Spider
- Miss Dolly had a Dolly
- Run, Run as Fast as You Can

- Cross Your Heart and Hope to Die
- Peek-a-Boo I See You
- Tweedledum and Tweedledee
- Easy as One, Two, Three
- There's No Place like Home
- Slenderman
- Where the Wild Roses Grow
- Waltzing Mathilda
- Drip Drop Dead
- Black Frost

JACK RYDER SERIES

- Hit the Road Jack
- Slip out the Back Jack
- The House that Jack Built
- Black Jack
- Girl Next Door
- Her Final Word
- Don't Tell

REBEKKA FRANCK SERIES

- One, Two...He is Coming for You
- Three, Four...Better Lock Your Door
- Five, Six...Grab your Crucifix
- Seven, Eight...Gonna Stay up Late
- Nine, Ten...Never Sleep Again
- Eleven, Twelve...Dig and Delve
- Thirteen, Fourteen...Little Boy Unseen
- Better Not Cry
- Ten Little Girls
- It Ends Here

MYSTERY/THRILLER/HORROR NOVELS

- IN ONE FELL SWOOP
- UMBRELLA MAN
- BLACKBIRD FLY
- TO HELL IN A HANDBASKET
- EDWINA

HORROR SHORT-STORIES

- MOMMY DEAREST
- THE BIRD
- BETTER WATCH OUT
- EENIE, MEENIE
- ROCK-A-BYE BABY
- NIBBLE, NIBBLE, CRUNCH
- HUMPTY DUMPTY
- CHAIN LETTER

PARANORMAL SUSPENSE/ROMANCE NOVELS

- IN COLD BLOOD
- THE SURGE
- GIRL DIVIDED

THE VAMPIRES OF SHADOW HILLS SERIES

- FLESH AND BLOOD

- Blood and Fire
- Fire and Beauty
- Beauty and Beasts
- Beasts and Magic
- Magic and Witchcraft
- Witchcraft and War
- War and Order
- Order and Chaos
- Chaos and Courage

THE AFTERLIFE SERIES

- Beyond
- Serenity
- Endurance
- Courageous

THE WOLFBOY CHRONICLES

- A Gypsy Song
- I am WOLF

DAUGHTERS OF THE JAGUAR

- Savage
- Broken

PROLOGUE
APRIL 2014

"The fourteenth of March. Hm...March is the third month. So that's three. That means we have one...and four...is five, plus three...and the year was nineteen-ninety-nine. So that is...twenty-eight. Add that to the five and three and you have...thirty-six. So that is three plus six and that equals...nine."

The numerologist looked at the number with satisfaction. Then she opened the book on the table next to her.

"So if her life path number is nine, then she is...," she put her pointer on the row of numbers and scrolled down till she reached the bottom. The numerologist frowned.

"Oh, that isn't good. Nine means you have a hard time letting go of the past. You are weighed down by the things you can't change. You often suffer from lack of sleep at night because you worry about tomorrow and your thoughts just wander off. You have an addictive personality. That's really bad. You depend on others to make you happy and when they don't, you might turn to drugs or alcohol. Let me take a look at your name. Maya was it? Let's see."

The numerologist flipped a page in her book and looked for the letters.

"Ah, here they are." The numerologist looked at the girl. "You do realize that the numerical value of your name influences areas of your personal and professional development in a huge manner, right? I really hope you do."

The girl whimpered. "Please, just let me go."

The numerologist stuck her finger in the air. "Shh, I'm trying to focus here. I'm here to help you, alright? You're out of balance and I need to figure out why. We need to figure out what motivates you, what causes all your trouble."

The girl cried harder now. "Please. I don't have any trouble. I'm not out of balance. You're the one who is out of balance. Please, just let me out of here."

"No," the numerologist said sounding very firm and angry. That was the only way to treat people who were in denial.

"Please, just let me go," the girl pleaded. "I can't stand being in here. I hate rats. I really hate rats. There's one in here with me inside this cage; it's crawling on me. I'm freaking out here. Pleeeaaase let me out."

The numerologist tried to shut out the girl's crying. She was tired of listening to her whine. Didn't she understand that this was much more important? Didn't she understand that she was only trying to help her? So many people walked through life without knowing why they were so miserable. It was all in the numbers. Why couldn't they see it the way the numerologist did? Why did they refuse to see it?

She focused on the book and the alphabet. "M is the number four and A is number one, so that's five. Y is a seven add that to the five you have twelve and then it ends with another A, so that's another one...so in total that gives us thirteen, so that is one plus three, that's four. Your name is a four...." The numerologist looked at the girl in the cage with a smile. "Isn't that interesting?"

"Pleease..."

"Four, huh?" she continued and flipped another page. "That means you're associated with *a foundation, order, service, struggle against limits, steady growth.* Hm...struggle against limits. Yes, that's certainly one of your problems. Hm and I sense a lot of negative energy associated with the name given to you at birth. Lots of anger. The numbers are certainly not working in your favor. You have a lot of ones in your name, but you need more threes and eights to balance you out. That's what we need to work on. The numerological vibrations of your current name are too negative the way it is now. See, the thing is, your numbers simply aren't compatible. Your life path number and your name number don't go well together. That's why you're having trouble in your life. That's why you tend to run away from home like you told me you did before you hit the poor guy with your dad's car. And stealing your father's car when you're only fifteen? That's really bad, Maya. Really destructive."

"You don't know anything about me," Maya hissed. She let out a scream and flipped the rat off her arm.

"Do be gentle with her," the numerologist said. "She's my family."

Maya grunted. "I don't care. Let me out of here or I'll kill it. I'll break its freaking neck."

The numerologist gasped. "Don't even joke about such a thing. This rat is very dear to me. I'm just trying to help you here, Maya. Four and nine are just not very compatible numbers. Don't you see? There is very little where the four and the nine see eye to eye. The problem is that they simply don't connect. The nine holds on to the past while the four wants to let it go. It's an eternal struggle inside of you and it's eating you up. We need to get you a new name and then everything will change. Everything will be better. I promise you."

The numerologist rose from her chair while mumbling to herself. "So how do we get more threes and eights into the poor girl's life? How to do it. What to name her? L is a three. Yes, we need some ones. And a Z, yes that's an eight. That's good."

The numerologist had an epiphany. She saw the name in front of her eyes like the universe had just sent it to her in a vision. She knew exactly what to call the girl. It was perfect. She walked to the desk and picked up a syringe. Then she walked towards the cage and opened the lock to the large rat cage that was the size of a small human. The rat squeaked and the girl whimpered as she saw the syringe.

"Please don't," she stuttered. She tried to fight her way out, but the numerologist overpowered her easily, then held her down and placed the needle on the skin of her shoulder and emptied its content into the girl's veins.

"It's okay. It's for the better...say goodbye to your old life, Zelllena."

1

APRIL 2014

"How can a fifteen year old girl simply vanish into thin air?"

I was yelling at the police officer in front of me, not caring one bit that everybody at the small police station in Karrebaeksminde had stopped talking and were now staring at me.

"She's been missing for three days now. There has to be something you can do. You have to have at least some idea of where she can be."

I felt Morten's gentle hand on my shoulder. He was trying to calm me down, but I didn't want to be calm. I had been looking for Maya for three days now—ever since I got back from Italy and still there was absolutely no trace of her."

"I know it's frustrating, Mrs. Frost, but we're doing all we can to find her," the officer I had come to know as Officer Hansen, told me. "Believe me, we want to find her as much as you do. She hit a man with a car and left him in the street. A hit and run is a very serious crime."

I sighed. I knew he was right. And, frankly, I couldn't believe my daughter would do such a terrible thing. If there was one thing I had taught her it was to own up to your responsibilities. You simply don't run.

"I know you're working hard to find her," I said and looked at Morten next to me. He had been such a wonderful help through it all. I had asked my parents take Victor with them back to the island as soon as we landed in Copenhagen after our disastrous cruise-trip. Morten and I had been staying in a hotel close to the police station in the small town ever since. The man Maya hit was in the hospital in Naestved, the closest big city, only a ten minute drive from Karrebaeksminde.

"I know we've been over this a couple of times," Officer Hansen said and cleared his throat. I could tell this case was beginning to get on his nerves. "But I need you to tell me again. What was your daughter doing in Karrebaeksminde anyway?"

I rubbed my forehead, thinking I was getting tired of answering the same questions over and over again.

"She wanted to get away from her father for some reason I have yet to get clarified. So she stole his car. I have no idea why she drove all the way down here. It's fifty-four miles from where her dad lives and more than a hundred and fifty miles from Fanoe where I live. It's not even on the way to Fanoe, so it appears she wasn't going back to the island. I have no idea where she could have been heading. She doesn't know anyone around here. She just moved back to her father's place in Copenhagen, so she hadn't made many friends before she decided to leave. I spoke to one of her new classmates yesterday, the only one that Maya had apparently been talking to at school, but she knew nothing of Maya's plans to leave. She never told a soul. And that worries me a lot. It's not like her to run away like this. It really isn't. As I told you before, I spoke with her on the phone while I was in Italy. It was right after the accident and I told her to call for an ambulance and then for her father to come and help her. But she never called me back. And she never called her father either."

"Well, I understand you're worried, but this is a typical pattern for a young criminal," Officer Hansen said. "She never called for an ambulance or her dad. She clearly didn't want to be caught. I've seen this many times before."

I shook my head in disbelief. "No. Not Maya. She's not like that."

"All parents say that," said the officer. It was one of those statements that it was impossible to argue against.

"I know it's hard to believe," he continued, "but these are the cold facts. She hit a man, then took the car and drove away. It's very simple."

"No," I said. "I don't think that's what happened. I'm afraid something bad happened to her after I spoke with her."

Officer Hansen looked troubled. "Well, as far as the police investigation goes, it appears she's run off and tried to hide from her actions. She'll show up at some point and then we'll take her in."

I exhaled. I knew there was nothing I could say or do to convince the officer. I had tried for three days now.

"So, why did you call us in again?" I asked. "I thought you had something new to tell me? First you tell me you have no clue where she is, then you call her a criminal. What's next? Did you just call us in here to insult us?"

"No, I didn't. As a matter of fact, we found something." The officer leaned backwards and pulled out a drawer. He picked something up and put it on the table in front of me. My heart literally dropped.

"Her phone?" I asked, as a million thoughts went through my mind. Maya would never abandon her phone, would she? No, never. She was a teenager. Her phone was her lifeline. "You found her phone?"

"It was thrown into a bush nearby where the accident happened. She probably threw it there herself when she decided to run from her crime...so we wouldn't track her down."

I gritted my teeth. It bothered me how he constantly referred to Maya as a crafty criminal. I knew in my heart she would never do such a terrible thing. I just knew it. The more I'd thought about it in the days after the accident, the more I had reached the conclusion that something had to have happened to her after I spoke with her. I simply refused to believe that Maya could have done this. And I had no intention of just waiting for her to show up on her own. I was going to find her, no matter the cost.

2

APRIL 2014

The first thing he noticed were the tubes. They were in his nose, but he couldn't see them. He could feel they were there. Next, there were the voices. There were people talking with low voices, serious voices, authoritative voices. Mads had no idea where he was and tried to open his eyes, but couldn't. He couldn't see anything and, no matter how hard he tried, he couldn't open his eyelids.

Had he gone blind? Panic spread inside of him. The voices in the room didn't seem to know he was awake.

The accident! I was in an accident. There was a car. Oh my God, I remember now. I was hit by a car.

Suddenly, he remembered in detail how the car had come closer so fast he couldn't react. He remembered thinking *this is it* before the car knocked him down. He even remembered the eyes of the girl behind the windshield. Those eyes had been so frightened, so terrified, right before she...before she drove right into Mads. He remembered the hit, the pain, and then his body rolling across the front of the car. He even remembered landing on the asphalt. He remembered seeing his own blood on the ground next to him. He remembered hearing the girl scream inside the car. He remembered a long time passed and he wondered what would happen next. He remembered the girl talking and crying. He remembered wondering if she would call for an ambulance. He must have been falling in and out of consciousness. The next thing he remembered was seeing her face close up. He remembered her looking at him. He remembered her reaching down and checking for a pulse. He clearly remembered her weary eyes when she realized what had happened. How did he remember all this?

Mads had no idea. He had to have been conscious at the time, he thought to himself, while pictures from the accident flickered inside of his mind. He saw the car again and again, moving towards him, then the pain, the scream, the girl, crying, then...then there was something else, wasn't there? There was someone there? He remembered seeing someone there before he lost consciousness.

Oh my God, I remember everything. There really was someone there. She took her. She took the girl. She forced her into the car and drove off with her, didn't she? Yes she did. I remember her standing there. I saw her. She walked closer; she looked at me, then at the girl. Then she hit her. Yes, that's what happened. She hit the girl with her fist, knocked her out, and then carried her to the car. Oh God, she hurt the girl. I have to tell someone, I have to tell...

Mads tried hard again to open his eyelids. He could still hear the voices in the distance, they were talking in a monotone, mellow fashion. Why weren't they helping him? Why weren't they aware that he was awake? They had to know. Didn't they?

Mads wanted to speak. He wanted to open his mouth and try to tell everything to the people in the room...tell about the girl and the woman and how he had seen everything. Even if he couldn't see them, they would certainly react when he started speaking.

But nothing happened. No matter how hard Mads tried, no words left his mouth. He didn't even open his mouth.

What the hell is this? What's going on?

"I am very sorry to have to tell you this, Mrs. Rahbek, but we believe that there isn't any hope for your brother."

Mrs. Rahbek? That's my sister! My sister is here. She can help me. Hey sis. I'm right here!

The male voice continued talking. "Mads was an organ donor. I do believe you and your mother should consider a transplant of his kidneys and liver."

"But it has only been three days?" His sister argued. "Couldn't he suddenly wake up from this coma? It has been known to happen before, hasn't it?"

"It has," the male voice said. "But in your brother's case, I don't believe he will wake up. There is no brain activity at all. I'm sorry. I'm not going to lie to you. There is no hope for him. We'll run some tests on his liver and kidneys to see if someone might be able to use them. I'm so sorry, Mrs. Schou."

Mrs. Schou? Mom? That's my mother. My mother is here? Why are they talking about me in the past tense? Why is the man saying there is no hope? There is lots of hope. I'm right here, Mommy, I can hear everything you're saying. I'm not dead. I'm alive. I can hear everything! Stop them. Don't let them take my organs. I need them. I'm alive. Hello? Can anyone hear me? Mommy, don't let them kill me. Don't let them!

"We'll probably need a few more hours before we make the final decision," Mads heard his sister say.

Yes, that's it, sis. Believe in me. I'm back. I'm here. I hear everything. You just need to see it. Look at me. I'm awake. I'm right here.

"His father is trapped in Dubai. He's trying to get on a plane to be here. We should at least wait to make our decision till he gets here, shouldn't we?" his sister continued.

No one answered. Mads wondered if his dad really was going to arrive to say goodbye. So many times in his life he had told him he was going to be there, but then forgot or ran into something more important.

"We've tried to reach Mr. Schou's wife," the male voice said. "We've left messages for her, but so far she hasn't been here. Do you have any way of reaching her? She might want to be able to say goodbye."

Say goodbye? What is he talking about? I'm not dead. I'm right here! Hello?

3

APRIL 2012

They were so happy on the day of their marriage. Mads and Signe were the couple everyone adored; they were the couple everyone looked up to and wanted to be like. From the outside, everything seemed to be perfect.

But as soon as the guests had left and Mads and Signe were once again alone, the quarreling began.

"The cake was terrible. It tasted like sweaty feet," Signe yelled. "How could you use that stupid baker from Rolighedsvej? I told you to go with the one from Nyvej. Don't you think I know why you chose her? Huh? You think I'm that stupid? You had a thing for her all along, didn't you?"

"For whom? The baker?" Mads asked.

"No. That girl who is behind the counter down there. Did you sleep with her? Did she put frosting in her bellybutton and have you lick it off, did she?"

"Ah, come on. That's ridiculous, Signe," Mads said. "But now that we're at it, don't you think I saw how you looked at Jacob during the reception? The way you tilted your head back and giggled every time he said anything. He's not that funny, you know. No one is. I was watching you the whole time while you spoke to him and looked at him with that little twinkle in your eye."

"Ah, shut up," Signe yelled. She grabbed her shoe and threw it at Mads. He ducked and it hit the wall behind him.

"Ha. Missed," he said with a grin. Then he picked up a book and threw it at her. It hit her on the shoulder.

"You're really bad at this," she said.

Mads laughed. Signe didn't. She was still angry and determined to show him. It had been a terrible wedding day. Well, not all the way horrible. There had been good moments as well. A lot of them, to be honest. She had enjoyed herself. It was just...well he just made her so jealous. She hated the way women looked at him. She was constantly afraid of losing him, some rich girl coming between them and sweeping him off his feet, making him realize that it was all wrong of him to marry her. That he deserved so much better.

Because he did. Signe knew he did. He was such a good man. A great catch and she was lucky to have him. But he could never know that. Of course he couldn't. He would be too sure of himself and stop fighting for her. That's what Signe's mother had always told her.

The moment they stop fighting for you, it is over. Men love the chase. Let him chase you. Keep it going. Never let him be certain of you.

So Signe made him fight for her constantly. And she was constantly jealous and afraid that someone better would come along and snatch him. She had to stay on her toes and could never rest.

"We should start packing for our trip to Egypt," Mads said, and picked up the shoe from the floor. "We need to be at the airport early in the morning."

Signe sat in a chair with a grunt and her arms crossed in front of her chest. "I'm not going," she said. "Not until you admit you like her."

Mads laughed again. "I'm not falling into that trap again. If I admit to that, you'll never go." He kneeled in front of her and took her hand. He kissed it. "So that's it?" he asked. "I'm damned if I do and I'm damned if I don't?"

Signe still didn't say anything. It was true that she had flirted with

Jacob. He was right about that. But that was only to make him jealous. She was terrified of the married life awaiting them. Now Mads knew for sure that she loved him. He knew where he had her. She belonged to him. Now he no longer needed to chase after her. It was over and it could only go downhill from now on. So she had decided to make sure he knew that he still had to fight for her. That she was still desirable to many men.

It had worked.

Mads came closer. He kissed her neck and whispered in her ear. "I was so angry seeing you with that guy. You wouldn't believe it. If it hadn't been my wedding, I swear to God, I would have…"

Signe stopped his kisses and looked at his face. "Would have what?" she asked.

"Killed him," Mads said. "If he had touched you in any way, I would have killed him right there on the spot."

Signe leaned back in the chair with a deep smile. She let him take her in the chair and enjoyed every grunt of desire coming from him.

"That's what I like to hear," she whispered. "That's exactly what I wanted to hear."

4

APRIL 2014

We left the police station feeling frustrated. I had hardly slept in days and felt exhausted. In Morten's car, I called my ex-husband Michael.

"They found her phone," I said, when he picked up.

Michael was quiet for a long while. I hoped he was feeling horrible for all that had happened and was blaming himself. I didn't tell him, but I was secretly blaming him. Maya had been in his care and under his supervision when all this happened. I couldn't understand how things could have gotten this far out of hand without him noticing it. Maya was the type who told you if something was wrong. She didn't just run off without a reason. But Michael had no idea what the reason was, he kept telling me. Either that or he wouldn't tell me. I was still indecisive on that subject.

"So what does that mean?" he asked.

"I have no idea. They still think she ran off after hitting the guy with the car. Officer Hansen seems to think she threw the phone away in order for them not to be able to trace her. I just don't think Maya is that cunning. I don't think she would ever think about doing that, do you?"

"I...I don't know, Emma. I haven't been with her much the past few years. I have to admit, I'm not sure I know her that well anymore. She did steal a car. My car. I don't know what else she is capable of."

I felt anger rise in me as Morten drove down the road. "What is that supposed to mean? You think she did this, don't you?"

Michael was quiet again. I didn't like his silence. It felt uncomfortable. How could he say these things about our daughter?

"What happened to you?" I asked. "You used to be such a nice guy and now this? What the hell happened to you?"

"I guess I've grown up," he said. "And so has Maya. Maybe it is time you realize she's no longer your little innocent daughter. She's almost a full grown woman with a will of her own, who makes her own choices. And right now she has made a really bad one. One that will cost her dearly. There really isn't much we can do about it."

Morten sensed I was agitated and put his hand in my lap. I snorted at Michael. "You've got to be kidding me, right?"

"Listen, I have to go…

"No. Michael. I'm not letting you go this easily. She's your daughter too. She needs you. Something happened to her after I spoke with her on the phone. I just know it. She needs the both of us right now. You need to be here for her."

I felt desperate. I couldn't stand him abandoning his daughter like this. I sensed he was pulling away more and more and I couldn't live with that.

"Emma. I'm married now. I have a wife and a child. I have a new family. I have a career. I simply don't have the time…"

"No. No. No. You don't. You don't pull out of this. You help me find her, do you hear me? You are going to help me."

"I can't…I have obligations. Victoria is…Maya isn't even…I mean she's not even my daughter, is she?"

"You're the only dad she has ever known."

"I really can't…"

So you're backing out. Is that it, huh? Is that how you want it to be?"

I looked at Morten who gave me an appalled look. He snorted loudly and mumbled something to himself. I was almost about to cry in anger and frustration when Michael suddenly hung up with a short statement:

"Keep me posted if there's any news."

I stared at the phone, trying to hold back tears and anger. Meanwhile, Morten drove the car into the parking lot in front of the hospital. He parked it and turned off the engine. Then he looked at me.

"Can you believe this guy?" I asked.

Morten shook his head. Then he leaned over and kissed me gently. It felt nice and made my worries diminish for just a split second. I sighed deeply.

"We don't need him," he whispered.

"We don't," I said. "But Maya does. She needs her father."

5

APRIL 2014

M ads was scared. No, it was worse than that. He was terrified. What had happened to him had, by far, surpassed his most horrifying nightmare. He couldn't believe this was happening. He couldn't believe it wasn't a dream. He kept yelling and screaming inside of his darkness, but none of it ever reached the people in the room with him.

Everything remained inside his head. There were times when he wondered if this was hell. If he had really died and this was his punishment for all the bad things he had done in his life.

But then he heard voices from the outside breaking through his darkness and filling him with hope.

No. No. This is real. They are real. I'm real. I'm alive. I can think. I can hear. I even believe I could see if only I could open my eyelids. I can see the light, can't I? I can see shadows outside and light coming through my eyelids, can't I? Or am I imagining it? No, it's real. Everything is real. My nightmare is real.

He could hear his sister's voice next to him. She was speaking to him, telling him how much she loved him and how she knew their dad would tell him the same if he had been there, if he hadn't been stuck in Dubai on that business trip. Now she was grabbing his hand and holding it in hers. He could feel her. He could feel the warmth of her hand. She was crying.

"You always were a spoiled brat," she said with a half-choked chuckle. "My God, how we could fight over things, Mads. But I still loved you. I always did. I even miss fighting with you already."

And I love you, sis. But I'm not dead. It doesn't have to end here. We can still fight. I would love to fight with you again. Let's do it right now. Right here and right now. I can come up with something to annoy you with. I know I can. Please don't give up on me, please don't.

Mads felt his sister touch his face. He heard her sob. "I can't believe he's really gone, Mom. It's so unfair. My baby brother shouldn't go before me. At least not now. Not this early. We just started our grown-up lives. We were supposed to have children at the same time. Our children should have grown up together."

"I know, darling. But I'm afraid we have to face that he's gone," Mads heard his mother say. "There is nothing we can do. At least his organs will end up helping others go on with their lives. Some other family will have their son and brother back."

"It's not fair," his sister said, sobbing.

"I know."

"Shouldn't we at least wait for dad?" his sister asked.

Mads' mother sighed. "I don't think that's very fair to the families waiting for the organs."

"But...?" Mads' sister said.

"Let it rest, Thilde," his mother hissed. "Your brother is dead. Nothing is going to change that."

But I'm not dead. Can't you see that? Mads was yelling inside of his mind. He was screaming in panic. *I'm alive. I'm right here! Oh, my God. What do I do? How can I let them know that I'm here before it's too late? My hand. Yes, my hand. I have to give them a sign somehow. Squeeze her hand. Just squeeze it! It can't be that hard, can it?*

Mads focused all of his strength on squeezing his sister's hand, but no matter how hard he tried, he couldn't. Nothing happened. His hand simply refused to obey.

Try something else. Do something simpler. Move a finger. Just one finger.

Mads focused once again and this time it felt like something was different. It felt like he was moving it.

I'm doing it. I'm moving the tip of my pinky. Did you see that?

Mads waited with great anticipation to hear his sister say something.

Come on. Tell me you saw it. Tell me you saw me move my pinky?

Mads listened when his mother suddenly spoke up. "I think we should just do it. There is no reason to drag it out any longer. Someone needs new organs. You heard the doctor. Mads is never going to wake up again."

Noooo! I'm here. I was moving the tip of my finger. Didn't you see it? Couldn't you see me moving? Please, just look at my finger. Just look at it!

"I'm not ready yet," his sister said. "I can't do it. I'm still waiting for him to open those eyes and say something annoying. God, I wish I'd been nicer to him."

"Don't beat yourself up like that," his mother said.

"I know. It's stupid. It doesn't change anything. It's just hard not to, you know? I know I have to let him go. Let them run the tests, then."

"I think that's the right thing to do. Somewhere, someone is waiting to get new organs and we owe it to them not to delay it further. We owe it to Mads. He was, after all, the one who signed up to be an organ donor."

No. No. I didn't. I didn't mean it. I take it back. I regret it. I don't want them to take my organs. Pleeease don't let them cut me open while I am still alive. Oh my God. Am I going to feel it? Am I going to feel everything when they cut me open? Am I going to feel the fire eating through my body while they cremate me? Oh God!

Another voice filled the room and made him stop screaming. It was a voice Mads had never heard before. It was the voice of a woman.

"Hello, my name is Rebekka Franck. Journalist at *Zeeland Times*. This is Sune Johansen, my photographer."

6

APRIL 2014

I had been to the hospital in Naestved every day to see how the guy Maya hit was doing. Every day, I was hoping for improvement, but there had been none so far. He had been in a coma ever since they brought him in and every day that passed, the family slowly lost more hope. I was devastated knowing my daughter had caused this and had talked a lot with the sister and mother who had stayed at the hospital waiting for their son and brother to wake up. Today, I brought Mads fresh flowers that the mother took with a labored smile when I entered the room and handed them to her.

"Thank you," she said politely, but emotionless, before she found a vase and poured in water.

I hated the way the mother and sister looked at me. They tried hard not to show it, but they resented me for what had happened to Mads Schou. I couldn't blame them. Maya wasn't here, so who else could they blame? I was, after all, Maya's mother. I had raised her and, even if they didn't say it out loud, I could tell by their looks that they didn't think I had done a very good job.

Someone else was in the hospital room with them today, someone I had never seen before. She was with a tall guy wearing a camera around his neck. He had a Mohawk and wore all black clothes and big boots. The woman was speaking with the sister, Thilde Rahbek. Thilde looked upset as she spoke. The woman was writing on her notepad, taking notes of what Thilde was telling her.

"What's going on here?" I asked the mother.

"It's a journalist from *Zeeland Times*. Thilde is just telling her the story of what happened. They're doing a story on the hit-and-run for tomorrow's paper," Mrs. Schou said.

I felt a pinch in my heart, knowing Maya's name would end up in the paper. It didn't feel good. Everyone would think she was a criminal.

"Any news about Mads?" I asked.

Mrs. Schou sniffled. "No. The doctor told us today that he probably won't wake up. He's an organ donor. They need to run some tests to see who he will be a fit for. I...It's all really just a little too..."

"I'm so sorry," I said, seeing the old woman's eyes tear up. She tried to hide it. "I really am."

She looked at me like she didn't really believe me. I knew she was secretly blaming me. It was brutal. The following silence was painful.

"So the girl who was driving the car ran off immediately afterwards?" I heard the journalist-woman say.

"Yes," Thilde answered. "Apparently, she had stolen the car from her parents. I don't know why they didn't know or at least know what was going on with her. But, as far as I know, the girl ran off from home, stole her parent's car and ran into my brother as he was crossing the road."

"So, you blame the parents?" The journalist woman asked.

She was starting to annoy me. It wasn't her job to make that kind of assumption.

"Of course I do. She was driving without a driver's license. She is fifteen. There's no reason she should be able to get ahold of car keys and take off. If her parents had kept a decent eye on her, this would never have happened. But apparently, the parents weren't even at the house when she took the car."

"Excuse me," I said.

Thilde and the journalist-woman both turned to look at me. "Yes?" the woman said.

"This is the girl's mother," Thilde said. "Emma Frost, this is Rebekka Franck. She's a journalist doing a story on the accident."

"Emma Frost? The author?" Rebekka Franck asked. "I love your books."

"Well yes, thank you, but there's no need to put my name in your little paper," I said.

Rebekka Franck put a hand in the air. "No, no. Of course not. I won't. This is Sune. He is my photographer."

The tall guy lifted a long arm and waved at me. "He will take some pictures of Mads, if that is alright with the family," Rebekka said.

"It is," Thilde said.

Rebekka Franck turned to look at me. "So you're the parent of Maya Frost. What do you say to the accusations from Thilde Rahbek just now?"

"Well, first of all, Maya was supposed to be with her father," I said. "We're divorced and I was on vacation in Italy when all this happened. Her dad was at his office across town. There was one adult in the house, her stepmother, but she didn't see Maya take the keys, since she was taking care of her newborn baby. Maya has had a hard time lately and recently moved to Copenhagen to live with her father. I've said this over and over again to the relatives, but I don't mind repeating it. I do not, for one second, believe my daughter would do anything like this. She called me right after it happened and she told me the man jumped out in front of her car. We agreed that she would call for an ambulance right away. She would never run away from her actions like this."

"But she never did," Rebekka Franck said curiously. "She never called for an ambulance. According to the police, it was a man passing with his dog later on who called for help. He later told the police that the car was fleeing the scene just as he arrived. He managed to see the license plate before it disappeared. But you still claim that your daughter would never flee? How do you explain it then?"

I could have killed the skinny little girl in front of me. Who did she think she was, coming here asking questions like that? The truth was that it had been my first thought when I received the call. That she had run away from it. But I didn't think that anymore. At least I didn't want to.

7

APRIL 2012

It was on the honeymoon in Sharm el-Sheikh in Egypt things started to go wrong for the young couple. They stayed in the honeymoon suite at a big resort outside of town and every day, after spending hours in the water snorkeling, looking at thousands of exotic and beautiful fish, they took a taxi downtown to go to dinner.

They liked the local food and the atmosphere in the streets and always ended up smoking water pipes in one of those small places where they put a Fez on your head and you sat comfortably on the ground on big velvet pillows.

It was all very perfect, they both agreed. Maybe a little too perfect. And it didn't take long before Signe started to get bored.

After a week in the small Egyptian town, she turned to look at Mads one night sitting on the red pillows. He was smoking a water pipe with a satisfied smile on his face.

"What's wrong?" he asked.

Signe tilted her head.

"You look like you just came up with a cunning plan or something," Mads continued. He laughed and smoked his pipe.

"I want to see other people," she said. She was as surprised by her outburst as he was.

Mads sounded like he was choking on the smoke and started coughing.

"What?" he asked when the worst of the coughing was over. "What did you say?"

"Nothing," she answered and drank her mint tea. It tasted the same as it had the day before and the day before that.

"Are you sure?" he asked.

"It was just a joke," she said.

Mads leaned back in his pillow. "Okay. Not a very good one, I must say."

"It was fun for me," she said. "Let's go."

Mads shrugged. "Why? Isn't it nice here?"

"No. I want to move on. I want to get drunk in a bar or something. Come on."

They paid and walked into the crowded street among the many western tourists. They were all so dull and boring, Signe thought. She saw an elderly couple walking towards them. Suddenly, everything inside of her screamed in despair.

That's us. That's us in like a hundred years from now. So this is it? Isn't there more to life than this?

"Let's do something crazy," she suddenly said and grabbed Mads' arm. "Come."

She dragged him down an alley and into a small bar with nothing but locals. They ordered two beers and sat in the back of the room.

"Why did you want to come here?" Mads asked.

Signe sipped her beer while staring at the bartender. He was young, in his early twenties. He was well-built and dark as the night.

"Look at him," she said.

"What about him?" Mads asked.

Signe sensed he was getting a little anxious now. It aroused her slightly. The feeling of utter power that she possessed over him.

"I want him," she said. "I want to fuck him."

"Are you kidding me?" Mads asked, appalled.

"Watch me."

Signe got up. She undid the top button of her dress so you could see the top of her breasts. With her beer in her hand, she walked to the counter and sat on a stool. The bartender smiled gently. His teeth were white against his dark skin. He was very handsome, she thought. He stared at her breasts.

"You like what you see?" she asked.

The man smiled and nodded. "Very nice."

"You want to touch? You want to fuck me?"

"Yes. Yes I do."

8

APRIL 2014

J ust like the previous nights, I couldn't sleep. I was walking around in the hotel room biting my nails and eating chocolate from the minibar while Morten slept in the bed. I stared into the night outside our hotel room. I saw hundreds of lights outside, coming from streetlamps or the inside of houses from people like me who couldn't sleep as well. I couldn't help but wonder if Maya was inside any of those houses...If she was somewhere nearby wondering how to get ahold of me. But why hadn't she called? Why?

Even if she ran, she knew I would forgive her. I would be angry, yes, but I was her mother. I would try and help her no matter what had happened. Didn't she know that? How could she not know that?

I am her mother goddammit!

I sulked a little and opened another chocolate bar. I ate it while hoping she at least was somewhere safe, that she wasn't wandering the streets somewhere or trusting the wrong people. It was terrifying to know she was out there for yet another night, alone without money or anyone to protect her.

She'll be back. As soon as she runs out of money, she'll be back. There's nowhere she can go, nowhere to stay. She'll call. Of course she will.

Her dad had told me she had taken around a thousand kroner from his drawer. It wouldn't last long. A couple of nights in a cheap hotel, and food for a couple of days, if she didn't eat much. That was it. She had to come back then. I had to cling on to that.

You don't really believe that, do you?

I didn't. I didn't believe for one second she was out there hiding somewhere wondering what to do next. I knew my daughter, for crying out loud. I couldn't let the police and that stupid reporter get to me.

"Aren't you coming to bed soon?" Morten asked with a drowsy voice.

"Sorry if I woke you up," I said and threw away the chocolate paper. I didn't want him to know that I was eating in the middle of the night. Not that he would have anything against it. I didn't think he would. No, I was just embarrassed. I hated that I couldn't stop eating whenever I felt agitated and worried.

"You're not helping Maya by staying up worrying all night," he said. "If we're to find her, then you need to be rested. Don't let all those stupid thoughts run off with you. They'll drive you insane if you let them."

I crawled into bed and cuddled up next to him. He put his arms around me. It felt good. I needed that.

"We'll find her. Don't worry, Emma," he said and kissed my forehead. "Now let's get some sleep."

I closed my eyes and finally dozed off. Once I had given in to the power of sleep and finally found my rest on some ship that could fly, my phone started to ring and woke me up.

"Maya!" I screamed and sprang out of bed. I answered the phone without looking at the display. "Maya?"

The voice on the other end was male. "No. I'm sorry to disturb you at this late hour, Mrs. Frost."

"Officer Hansen?" My heart stopped. I was strained by fear. Why was he calling like this in the middle of the night? Had something happened? Had they found Maya? Oh no, had something bad happened to her?

Please tell me she is alright.

"What's going on, Officer?" I asked with a shivering voice. My eyes met

Morten's. He was worried as well. As a police officer, he knew they only called when really bad things happened.

"We found the car," Officer Hansen said. "I thought you should know."

"The car? Where?"

"In the fjord. It's being pulled up as we speak. Divers have been down there and they saw the license plate. I just received word. I thought you should know."

I gasped. I focused on keeping my breathing steady. "...and...and Maya?"

"She wasn't in it. The car was empty."

9

APRIL 2014

I was hardly breathing when I hung up with Officer Hansen.

"They found the car?" Morten asked.

"They're pulling it out of the fjord as we speak," I said.

Morten got up from the bed. He threw my jeans at me and put his shirt on. "Let's go."

"Go where?"

"To wherever the car is being pulled out. If we're going to find Maya, then we need all the clues. They might pull something out of the car that can point us in her direction."

I wasn't going to argue against that. I wasn't going to sleep anyway and I really wanted to go and see the car. I got dressed and we drove towards the harbor while Morten made some phone calls to find out where it was exactly they had found the car. Sometimes, it really paid off to be the girl-friend of a police officer. I felt very blessed to have him as I listened to him find out internal things I would never be able to on my own. I couldn't believe he had taken a week off from work to help me search for Maya. He had done so without even blinking. "It's the least I can do," was his response when I thanked him.

I didn't think it was.

"My colleagues told me they think the car was driven into the water from the bridge to Enoe. They're pulling it out of the water from the harbor in Karrebaeksminde on the landside of the bridge. I should be able to get us in behind the police barricade."

"You're the best," I said.

Morten drove us through the small town of Karrebaeksminde, then parked the car at the harbor. It was very easy to find the scene. They had lit the entire area up with lamps, and huge cranes were working on pulling Michael's car out. Just as we arrived, I spotted it hanging in the air and the crane was now turning to get it back on land. We walked to the police tape and Morten talked to the officer there, showing him his badge and telling him I was a person of interest who needed to be there.

It wasn't far from the truth.

Morten walked in front of me towards the car that was now being carefully placed on the asphalt with a loud clunk. My heart was in my throat as I looked at the wrecked car and at all the water that was now splashing out of it onto the ground. Up until now, it had all been like an odd dream, like a freakish nightmare, but seeing my ex-husband's car in front of me suddenly made it all seem very real. I gasped for air and felt Morten's hand on my shoulder.

"It's okay, Emma," he whispered. "She wasn't in it, remember. She's still out there somewhere. She's still alive. Don't lose hope. Without hope you'll never be able to find her."

I caught my breath and bent over slightly in order to breathe better. I watched as forensics experts attacked the car and started securing evidence. I heard the sound of a camera clicking behind me and turned to see Rebekka Franck and that photographer of hers. They had somehow managed to get past the police barricade as well. She saw me and came closer. I sighed and turned my head away. I really didn't want to speak to her right now.

"Emma Frost?" she asked. I could hear her footsteps approaching. I didn't turn to look, but knew she was right behind me. "Oh my God, Emma, how are you feeling?" she asked.

Startled by her compassion, I turned to look at her.

"It must be awful for you," she said.

"Well...Wait. Is this for your paper?" I asked, suddenly afraid of making the front cover with some dramatic headline.

"No. No. Of course not. I mean, we're going to mention that the car was found and pulled out of the water, but I'm not going to mention a word about you. I see no reason to."

I felt relief. Maybe she wasn't as hungry for sensation as I had first taken her to be. "Well, good. 'Cause this is kind of private."

"I know. Oh my God, no. I don't do that kind of journalism. I was just thinking about you. I have two kids of my own. I can't imagine what you must be going through."

"I don't think most people would want to," I said. I felt the tears pressing behind my eyes, but refused to let them go.

"At least there was no one in the car," Rebekka said. "Gives you hope that she is still alive, right?"

I nodded. I didn't feel like talking anymore. This was simply too hard. I knew if I opened my mouth, I would burst into tears. I heard someone shout and turned to look in the direction of the car. A guy in a blue bodysuit had found something and was holding it in the air.

I gasped and grabbed hold of Morten's shirt.

"What is it?" Rebekka asked. "What did they find? It looks like a necklace of some sort."

"It's Maya's necklace." I said and looked at the golden chain with the heart hanging from it. The heart with the four small diamonds in it that I had seen so many times when looking at my daughter.

10

APRIL 2012

The bartender followed her into the bathroom in the bar. They passed Mads on the way and Signe gave him a flirtatious look.

"Signe, goddammit," he said, but she danced past him like she hadn't heard him, like it was the most natural thing in the world for her to walk to the restroom with a strange man.

Signe opened the door and signaled the bartender to follow her. Just as she closed it, her eyes met Mads' and she could have sworn his eyes turned black. It amused her. She liked seeing him like this. It wasn't that she cared about the bartender. No, she was indifferent about him. No, what aroused her was the tension, the excitement of knowing she had made her husband green and flaming with jealousy.

She pulled the bartender closer and let him kiss her neck. She moaned purposely loud to make sure Mads could hear them. The bartender smelled like sweat and he had bad breath when he kissed her. She felt his hand up under her skirt and his fingers finding their way underneath her panties.

"Oh yes, bad boy," she moaned. "Take me. Touch me right there. I want to feel you inside of me. I want to feel your big cock inside of me now. I bet you have a huge cock, don't you?"

The bartender smiled and opened his pants and let it out. Signe was disappointed. It was small, probably the smallest she had ever seen. It made her angry with him. The bartender grabbed her by the waist and pulled her closer.

"Now, we make love," he whispered in her ear.

Where is he? Where is Mads? Why isn't he doing something?

Signe moaned louder and giggled as she felt the bartender's hands all over her breasts. He was fumbling and hurting her slightly. But it was all worth it, knowing Mads was out there being eaten up with jealousy. This would teach him not to take her for granted.

"Easy there, tiger," Signe said, as the bartender grabbed her hands and held her up against the wall.

"You say we fuck, I say we fuck," the bartender said in his bad English. "So now we fuck."

"I think I might have changed my mind," Signe said. It hadn't been her intention to go through with it anyway. She just wanted to add a little excitement to the vacation. To spice it up a little. She wanted Mads to burst in there and tell her not to go through with it. But he wasn't coming, was he? Had he given up that easily? Wasn't he prepared to fight for her after all? Maybe he didn't love her as much as he had pretended to?

"Please, get off me," Signe said and tried to pull her hands loose, but the bartender held her tight.

"We fuck," he said.

"No. No we don't," Signe said "I changed my mind."

The bartender shook his head. "No. We fuck now."

He held her hand in a tight grip and was pushing himself at her when suddenly the door to the restroom opened and Mads stormed in. Signe smiled widely when she saw him. Then she closed her eyes and pretended to be enjoying the bartender's touch.

"Oh yes, right there, give it to me bad boy. Give it to me."

"Signe!" Mads yelled. "Stop it and come back with me. Don't do this to us."

She opened her eyes and looked at her husband. She was thrilled to see the anger in his eyes. "Fight for me," she said.

"What?"

"Fight for me or I'll let him fuck me. You hear me Mads? I want you to fight for me. Hurt him."

Mads, who was at least two heads taller than the Egyptian guy didn't think it over for even a second. He grabbed the bartender by the neck and pulled him away from Signe, forcing the Egyptian guy to smash against the wall. Then he punched the bartender in the face and the blow made the guy fall backwards into the porcelain sink with a loud thud.

After that, the bartender didn't move anymore. Mads looked at Signe. Her eyes grew wide. "He's not moving, Mads. His head is bleeding. Is he... Do you think he...?"

Mads bent down and felt for a pulse, then he looked up at Signe.

"Yes, he's dead."

"You killed him? You killed him...for me?" Never had Signe loved her husband more than she did in those seconds.

11

APRIL 2014

They kept the necklace. The police told me it was evidence and put it in a small plastic bag to be examined. Morten and I watched as they pulled the car apart and then we decided to go back to the hotel. Rebekka Franck and her photographer also left after having taken a few pictures and taken a statement from the police. She waved to me as she walked back to her car and I waved back. She still annoyed me, but there was something about her I had started to like. She seemed honest and fair. And very professional.

The next morning, when I read the local paper on my iPad in the hotel restaurant, I found her article to be very decent and fair towards us. Maya didn't come off as just a criminal. It was put up to the reader to judge. Rebekka had taken the statements from the police and the sister Thilde, but made sure to write that there were still doubts about what really happened to the girl who drove the car that hit Mads Schou.

I was satisfied with the outcome. I wouldn't say I was happy, because I don't think you'd ever be happy to see your daughter's name mentioned in this context, but I wasn't angry with it. It was fair.

I grabbed another croissant from my plate, put some jam on it and ate it. Morten sipped his coffee. I felt disgusted with myself. I had eaten almost all night and here I was at it again. It just showed me how devastated I really was. Morten noticed it as well.

"It's okay to be upset, Emma," he said. "You can tell me if you're sad. You don't have to keep hiding it from me and trying to be this superwoman. I know you worry. And I know you eat a lot when you worry."

I took another bite of the croissant. I felt embarrassed. "You're right. You have no idea how much I've eaten the last couple of days," I said.

"I think I have a slight idea," he said. "I've been with you, remember? Now, I don't care that you eat a lot, not even that you eat a lot of chocolate at night. You're beautiful to me, no matter what happens and I know it's just because you're upset. But I worry about you. I'm afraid you're making yourself more and more miserable because you don't talk to me about things that bother you. It's like you shut everything off inside of you. And then you stuff your mouth to keep it down."

Where did I find this guy? Did he eat something, a pill or something in childhood to make him always say and do the right things? How can he be so sensitive and understanding?

"Are you for real?" I asked.

Morten chuckled. "What do you mean?"

I shook my head. "Nothing. It's just that sometimes it's hard to believe in things that are too good to be true. That's all."

He looked confused. I realized I should just shut up now. "Thank you," I said. "Thank you for understanding me. And I promise I will try to be more open with you. It's just not something I'm very used to. I grew up drowning all my emotions with food. If my parents had a quarrel or even a disagreement, my mother would be in the kitchen all afternoon cooking all of my dad's favorites. By dinnertime, he would have forgotten all about it. We all would. We never liked to talk about things. We just ate till it went away on its own. I guess it means we had a lot of oppressed emotions, huh?"

"Sounds like it," Morten said and finished his coffee.

I looked at the croissant and put the rest back on my plate. I was stuffed anyway. There was no reason to finish it. I looked at Morten when my phone suddenly rang. I looked at the display and didn't recognize the number.

"Emma Frost."

"Rebekka Franck here."

"Good morning, Rebekka," I said, startled. She was the last person I had expected to call me.

"Well it might be morning to you, but I've been up for hours. That's just the way it is when you have a one-year old, huh?"

I could vaguely remember. I had hated that time with the little ones when you were up all night and had to get up early in the morning. All of a sudden, I missed it for some reason. I missed holding Maya in my arms and knowing that she was safe.

"What can I do for you Rebekka?"

"To tell you the truth, I didn't sleep at all last night after we got back from the scene at the harbor. Not because of the baby or the article, no it was something you said that got me thinking. Could you come by my office at the paper today?"

I looked at Morten. We hadn't decided what we would do today. We had discussed going back to Maya's school one more time to talk to her friend but we had already talked to her twice and I didn't think there was anymore to be gained from her.

"We'll be right there," I said and hung up.

12

APRIL 2014

I did some research on Rebekka Franck in the car on our way to her office in Karrebaeksminde. To my surprise, she wasn't just some local reporter. She had made it big time once. She'd been a correspondent for the country's biggest newspaper and been to Iraq and Afghanistan. But that was all like ten years ago. Now, she had apparently given all that up and taken a job as a small-town reporter for a medium-sized newspaper that covered all of Zeeland, the island containing—among other things—our capital of Copenhagen. Apparently, she had started out as a reporter only for the local news in Karrebaeksminde, but now she was covering all of the island. She was their star-reporter and often delivered the scoops that made the front cover. She'd had her share of strange cases and even several times solved mysteries that the police had given up on.

Her office was situated on the first floor of an old building in Karrebaeksminde. It was small, to my surprise. Only three desks. One for Rebekka, one for her photographer Sune and then a third for a secretary-type who greeted me and Morten and presented herself as Sara. I liked Sara right away. She was smiling and offered me a piece of cake. She went into a small kitchen and came back with coffee for all of us.

"Thank you Sara," Rebekka said to her co-worker, who went back to her desk and put on a set of headphones.

"Police scanner," Rebekka said and nodded in her direction. "Sara likes to listen in on the police's conversations. That way, we always know if something is going on and can be there on the spot. It's very effective."

"I see," I said and looked at Morten, who seemed slightly taken aback by the fact that someone might be listening in on him when he was at work.

"Morten is a police officer," I said.

"Well, it's not illegal," Rebekka said with a smile.

"That's true," Morten said and sipped his coffee. "But you won't be able to do it much longer. Most districts have started using new encrypted digital radios that you can't listen in on."

Rebekka chuckled and sipped her coffee. "True. They already have them in Aarhus where I used to work before I came here. But this is the countryside. It's going to take a while before the police get them out here."

I ate my chocolate cake while my thoughts wandered off. I really didn't care about police-scanners or whether they were digital or not. I couldn't stop worrying about Maya. A copy of today's paper was on the desk next to us. It had Maya's necklace and the car on the front cover. I felt a pinch in my heart thinking about my daughter. I never should have let her go live with her dad. I should have stopped her. I should have told her to stay with me. Then none of this would have happened.

"How are you, Emma?" Rebekka asked, all of a sudden.

I looked at her. I couldn't read her. Was she just being nice to me because there was a story for her to tell, or was she as sincere as she seemed? I didn't trust her. I never trusted journalists. I had worked on magazines myself and knew how driven they could be in getting their story, how heartless they could become in the chase. I had no idea if this woman was like that, but the fact that she had been the star reporter of the biggest newspaper in the country told me she had the sharp elbows and the drive. I never cared much for that. Plus, she was way too skinny for someone who just had a baby a year ago. I couldn't believe it. She looked great.

"I'm okay, I guess," I said. "I mean it isn't easy...Well, you know."

"That's why I thought that I might be able to help you," Rebekka said. "I have some experience in strange cases like this that the police have given up on or think they've already figured out. To me, there is something definitely wrong with this."

I was intrigued. Finally, someone who wanted to listen. "Yes? How do you figure that?"

"Like I said on the phone, it was something you said when I met you at the hospital that got me thinking. You told me your daughter said on the phone that the guy jumped out in front of the car. Were those the words she used? That he jumped?"

"Yes. She told me it wasn't her fault and that *someone jumped right out in front of the car*. There was nothing she could do. Those were her words."

Rebekka looked pensive. "Hm," she said.

"What are you thinking?"

"Well, I read the police report of the accident...Sune found it. He does things like that." Rebekka looked at Morten. "Maybe you shouldn't hear this."

Morten shook his head. "I'm here as a private person, not a police officer."

The photographer looked like he wasn't sure he believed him. Rebekka touched his hand. "Tell him what you saw, sweetie. It's okay."

The tall guy nodded. "Well, I read the entire report through, all the details, and what puzzled me...well, us...was the fact that there were no skid marks on the asphalt at the site."

"Really?" Morten asked.

"No," Rebekka said. "That can only mean one thing. Your daughter never saw what was coming or she would have tried to hit the brakes, right?"

"Naturally. She was so upset afterwards. I fear she might have gone into some type of shock. That has so far been my only explanation as to why she would have driven off. But I just don't understand why she hasn't called since, after the shock subsided. Why hasn't she come back? That's what scares me."

"That's understandable," Rebekka continued.

"So, what do you suggest we do?" I asked, hoping desperately she had some idea because I had none.

Rebekka leaned in over the table. "I was thinking that maybe we should look a little into that Mads Schou fellow."

"The guy in the coma?" Morten asked.

I was beginning to see what Rebekka was getting at.

"Who is he?" she asked. "And, more importantly, what was he doing jumping out in the street in front of a car like that? We can all agree he must have come suddenly, like out of the blue, right? Or else Maya would have hit the brakes. So, whether he jumped or walked is still unknown, but we can also agree that he can't have looked at where he was walking or maybe running. Why wasn't he paying attention to where he was walking before crossing the street? It was broad daylight. The car Maya drove was an SUV. It was big and noisy. What was this guy doing out there all alone? He could have been on his way to somewhere, he could have been out on a stroll. We don't know. But something is definitely off and I say we take a look at him and figure out what he was doing before he was hit by the car. It might be a long shot and we might not get anywhere with it, but I think it is worth a try, don't you?"

I looked at Rebekka Franck, feeling a slight ray of hope grow inside of me. "I'm in," I said. "I think it is a great idea."

"Good," Sune said. "I think I might be able to hack his social security number and get to know a lot about this guy. You know, if he was ever arrested, if he's been receiving social welfare, etc."

Rebekka looked at Morten, who tried hard not to be upset. "Still here as a private person," he said and held his hands resignedly in the air.

Rebekka laughed. "Good to hear. Well Sune is good with stuff like that. But he can't get caught, it's very important."

"I know a little myself," I said. "I can get pretty handy on a computer and have hacked into the police database several times as well."

Sune smiled. "I think I'm in love. Rebekka, move over, we have a winner," he said, laughing. He had a sweet and gentle laughter. I liked Sune right away and Rebekka was beginning to grow on me as well.

"Perfect. You two hit the computers. Morten, you work with me. I can use your expertise and contacts in the real world. Let's get to work."

13

APRIL 2014

The numerologist had put Zelllena in the back of her car and was now driving her to her new home. The numerologist was whistling while driving. Her iPod played the Jackson Five song ABC. She had always loved that song and played it over and over again.

"...A, B, C...It's easy as one, two, three," the numerologist mumbled. "As simple as do, re, mi, A, B, C, one, two, three."

She looked at Zelllena in the back seat. She was still heavily sedated. The poor girl had messed up her life. The numerologist was going to give her a new life, a fresh start in a place where the numerologist knew she would be able to keep a close eye on her. It was perfect.

The numerologist giggled at her own plan. It was so perfect, so flawless. She looked at the girl in the rear-view mirror again.

"Yes Zelllena, this is perfect for you. Where I'm taking you, you'll never be able to run away again. You'll never defy your parents again and hit someone with a car again. You know the police are looking for you, don't you? I saw your picture in the paper this morning. If I don't help you, you'll end up in jail and I really don't think you deserve that. I think I can help you. I can give you a new start, a BRAND new life."

She had cut the girl's hair short and colored it blonde so no one would recognize her. She couldn't have the police finding her. She had also put new clothes on her...some things that were just lying around the house anyway. They fit her perfectly.

"It'll be our secret what you've done, won't it?" she asked and turned the car into a parking lot. She turned the engine off. The numerologist drew in a deep sigh of satisfaction. She looked at herself in the mirror and put on some red lipstick.

"You're a hero," she whispered to her own reflection. "Saving this girl from a life as a criminal is by far the best thing you have ever done. You know what happens to them once they are put in those awful prisons, don't you? Yes you do. You know better than anyone how they're treated and how their lives are destroyed. You know how she would meet bad, bad people in there who would teach her bad things. You know...You know...how they come at night...how they...how they...You know she's innocent. You saw what happened. You know it was an accident, but no one will ever believe you or the girl. Giving her a new life is the best thing you can do. You're her savior. You're a hero and should be celebrated as one. But they'll never know. They can never know. You have to hide her away. Yes, you do."

The numerologist froze at the memories in her mind. Pictures of nightly abuse and endless pain she couldn't escape. She shook her head and swallowed her tears. No, this certainly wasn't the time for self-pity. This was a happy moment. Saving this girl from a destiny worse than death, a destiny similar to the one she had suffered herself, was the best thing she could do. It was her mission. The numbers had told her so. It was written all over them.

"Threes. You're a three, remember?" she told her reflection and closed her eyes. "Threes are joyous people. They are people that others are drawn to. They're creative, they're fun to be with. You're a three, remember."

The numerologist clenched her fists till it hurt and repeated the number. "Three, three, three."

Who are you trying to fool? You're a seven, remember? You can't run from that.

"No. No. No, it's not true. I'm not anymore. I don't like sevens. They're shy and introverted. I'm nothing like that!"

The numerologist held her hands to her face, pulling her hair. "No," she said sobbing slightly. "I'm not a seven."

She pulled herself together and looked at the girl again. She looked so peaceful while sleeping. The numerologist heard voices outside her car as four men came running out of the building. She forced a smile as they opened the door. A man looked inside.

"Is this her?"

"It is. She's sedated, so she shouldn't cause much trouble."

"We'll take care of her from here on out," the man said and grabbed Zelllena by her arms and hands. He pulled her out of the car where the other three men helped him carry her inside. The numerologist watched with a tear in the corner of her eye as Zelllena disappeared into the building.

"It's the right thing to do, Zelllena. Trust me on this. You're safe now. No one will ever be able to find you here."

14

APRIL 2012

"**D**ID YOU SEE THAT?"
        Signe looked at Mads with excitement. He seemed troubled and kept looking behind him to see if anyone was following them. They jumped into a taxi and drove to the hotel. "It was awesome," Signe said, as they went back into their room. "I mean, he had no idea what was coming and then you just hit him like this!"

Signe swung her fist through the air to make it look like Mads had when he hit the bartender. Mads sat on the bed. Signe climbed up on his lap. She held his face between her hands.

"Do you have any idea how sexy you are to me right now?" she asked.

"Signe. I killed the guy," Mads said. "I'm terrified of ending up in some Egyptian prison. Can't you see that?"

"But Mads. He was raping me, don't you remember? He was holding me by the neck and wanted to rape me. You're my hero. You fought for me." She leaned over and kissed him. They fell backwards on the bed and soon she was all over him. She grabbed his shirt and pulled it off. Never had she wanted him more in her life.

"Take me, Mads. Use those strong hands that just killed a guy to take me," she moaned.

"You're insane, do you know that?" he asked and rolled around till he was on top of her.

She laughed manically. Mads smiled and leaned over her and kissed her. "My crazy wife," he whispered, then put his hand up under her dress. "When I saw you today with that guy, it made me so angry. So jealous...you have no idea. I wanted to kill him. I wanted to beat the crap out of him and I wanted to fuck you right there on the spot afterwards. You're a crazy bitch, but I like it. You scare the shit out of me, but it arouses me." Mads grabbed her by the neck and blocked her breathing for a little, then let go.

Signe gasped for air and coughed.

"I could kill you as well, right here and now," he whispered.

Signe moaned. Her body writhed underneath him. "Fuck me, killer. Fuck me while trying to strangle me."

Mads grabbed her neck and entered her while blocking her breathing again. She was struggling underneath him and it made him go at her even faster, even harder. When her face turned red, he loosened his grip slightly to let her breathe. She moaned and groaned and she sailed into an orgasm like none he had ever given her before. He held her down and came right after.

Then he let her go. He fell to the side with a deep moan. Signe was gasping for air and panting. When she caught her breath, she started laughing. Mads laughed as well.

"I love you," he said and turned to look into her eyes.

"I love you too. Let's get out of here."

"We still have two weeks left of our honeymoon. Are you sure?" Mads asked.

Signe nodded. She was tired of this place. It was already getting boring again. "Yeah. We had our fun. It's time to move on. Plus, I don't want to have to deal with the police in case they come knocking on our door."

Mads sighed, satisfied. "Where do you want to go? Home?"

"No. Let's go somewhere exciting. Somewhere fun. I was thinking we could go to Turkey. I have never been. I hear Alanya should be fun."

"Well, we still have the money my parents gave us as a wedding gift to buy a house," Mads said. "We could use a little of that if we need to. Just buy a smaller one, maybe?"

An idea was shaping in both of their minds. One that wouldn't be popular with Mads' wealthy parents, but that just made it even more fun, now didn't it?

To Signe it did. She knew how Mads' mother felt about her not being good enough for her son and about them getting married when they were only nineteen. His mother was the one who ran the show when it came to family affairs. She had controlled Mads all of his life and Signe knew how much it had bothered her that she was no longer able to control him. So now that they had decided to get married anyway, the mother insisted on making all their decisions including choosing a house for them to live in.

"We don't need no stinking house," Signe said.

15

APRIL 2014

Rebekka let me use her computer. I stared into the screen, not knowing where to start. I had no idea who this guy was. All I knew was that his name was Mads Schou and, as far as Rebekka had told me, he belonged to a very wealthy family who lived in Karrebaeksminde in one of the old villas by the sea.

Sune was going to take care of all the official stuff, like searching for him in the police database, so where did that leave me?

Well I started out by finding him on Facebook. I searched his name and found several by that name, but only one located in this area. I opened his profile. A nice picture of him from his wedding day was the first thing I saw. It was his cover photo. His profile picture showed a close-up of his face, smiling and looking nothing at all like the guy I had seen in the hospital every day since my daughter disappeared.

He was young and quite handsome. I scrolled and saw posts by others stating they heard about the accident and how sorry they were for what had happened to him and that they hoped he would be okay. His settings were very private so I couldn't see any of his other pictures unless I became Facebook friends with him. I scrolled through his profile again and tried to go into previous posts, but couldn't do that either. Not knowing what else to do, I decided to try and log into his account. I couldn't guess his password, so I used my hacking skills that I had learned from an old boyfriend and got access to his account. It was surprisingly easy.

I looked up from the screen and my eyes met Morten's. He was on the phone talking to someone from the police. Rebekka was right next to him. I really hoped they were getting somewhere. I didn't feel like I was.

I scrolled his page and looked at all his posts. He wasn't one to post a lot of stuff. Mostly his posts were about his favorite soccer team—Liverpool. I looked through his pictures and saw lots of pictures from his wedding. Signe Schou was his wife's name. Why hadn't I met her in the hospital? It was always the sister and the mother who were there. I didn't understand that. On his profile, it said they were still married, so it wasn't like they had divorced. Besides, they had only been married two years. Where was she?

I wrote her name, followed by a question mark on a piece of paper next to me, then continued through his profile. I would check her out later. Now I was looking for anything that could tell me what he was doing on the day he was hit by the car.

The latest post he had made was the day before the accident. It simply said YNWA. It was posted on Signe Schou's wall. Apparently, she had posted the same on his the next day. I looked at it, then at Sune.

"Do you know what YNWA means?"

"You'll never walk alone," he answered. "It's a signature for Liverpool fans. You know, the English soccer team?"

"I know," I said disappointed. I had hoped it meant something important. "It was Mads Schou's last post on Facebook on the day before the accident."

Sune nodded. "So he's a Liverpool fan, huh?"

"Guess so. Seems to be all he posts about. That and pictures from his wedding two years ago."

"Interesting," Sune said and returned to his screen. His fingers were dancing rapidly across the keyboard. I looked at it, impressed. I had never seen anything like it. I stared at the profile picture and suddenly felt like I was wasting my time. I should be out there in the world looking for Maya instead of going through this guy's private stuff.

I went back to the front page and looked at it. I leaned back wondering what it was about this guy and his pictures that annoyed me.

Then, something caught my eye. I leaned forward and clicked on "Events." Maybe twenty events showed up...birthday parties, weddings, cocktail parties and so on. But one in particular caught my eye.

"Bingo," I said.

Sune looked up again. Rebekka came towards me. Morten followed her.

"You got something?" Rebekka asked.

"Look at this. This event is dated for the day when he was hit by the car."

Rebekka came closer, then read the invitation out loud:

"Murder Party?"

"That's what it says," I said.

Rebekka continued to read: "Only for the invited. A murder will take place on April 19th 2014 at noon in the old theater in Karrebaeksminde."

Rebekka looked at me. "What the hell is a murder party?"

I shrugged. "Maybe it's like those murder game parties. They're often used as fundraisers. They turn off the lights and then someone is tapped on the shoulder and has to fall to the ground and then when the light is turned back on the others are supposed to guess who did it. Something like that," I said. "There's an old novel written about it too...an old Miss Marple mystery."

"Whatever it is, it looks like it is where Mads Schou might have spent his last hours on Saturday the 19th," Rebekka said. "If you look here, he accepted the invitation and said he was going to participate."

16

APRIL 2014

They were running tests on him. Mads could feel it when they stuck their needles in his skin and took blood samples; he could hear them talking amongst each other, some of the nurses were even making jokes while taking samples from his body.

And he couldn't do a damn thing about it. He was stuck inside of his own body and couldn't tell a soul he was still alive. Still, Mads was clinging to a tiny ray of hope. Mads had moved his pinky. He was certain he had. It had felt different than when he tried to move anything else and it didn't react. The pinky reacted. It really did. It might not have been much motion, since no one seemed to notice, but it was something. Now he only wondered if he would be able to get them to notice before they cut him open and took his organs.

His mother and sister hadn't come yet. Mads had no idea of time or date. He only knew it was daytime, since the room was constantly filled with nurses and doctors and it was never like that at night when everything went frighteningly quiet and all he could hear was his own thoughts.

Now he heard a nurse come in the room and he listened to her clogs as she walked across the linoleum floor. Mads had learned the sounds pretty well by now. He knew the difference between them in the way they walked. He used the rhythm in their steps, the sound of their shoes, things rattling in their pockets, humming voices or whistling, or just the way someone cleared his throat to distinguish between them. That's how he knew the person approaching now was a woman. By the sound of her clogs. She was very tall, he guessed. Her steps were far apart and he guessed she had very long legs. Mads focused all of his strength on moving his pinky again and, this time, he was determined that she should see it. She just had to.

She was almost by his bedside now. She stopped and he guessed she was checking his monitor and the fluid next to him. She changed the bag of fluids that kept him hydrated, then pressed a button on the monitor to make sure his heart rate was okay. Mads knew her every move. Six times a day they did the same routine. Then she wrote the numbers down on his chart and hung it on his bed. Mads moved his pinky all he could to signal her that he was awake. Usually when they were done with the chart, the nurses left and it would be hours before anyone came back, unless they were doing more tests. Mads tried all he knew how to. He was certain the finger had to be flipping in the air by now, with all the strength he was putting into it. Then something extraordinary happened. While Mads was expecting to hear the steps of her leaving the room to attend other patients, she didn't. Instead, she paused. He listened carefully, but heard no steps, no movement whatsoever. Could it really be? Was she looking at him?

Please see it. Look at my finger. Please see me!

More steps. They weren't walking away. They were approaching. Mads couldn't believe it. She was coming closer. With great excitement, he listened to her steps while moving the fingertip as much as he could. He was getting tired now, but the desperation kept him going.

Please just see it. Please?

The nurse stopped. She was being very quiet now. He sensed that she was close. He could feel her warmth. He could hear her breathing. Was the sound coming closer? Was her breathing coming closer to him? Was she leaning down towards him?

She's seen it. She must have seen it!

Mads felt her warm breath on his skin. She was close to his ear now.

Was she examining him? Was she going to say something? Had she realized he was awake and now was checking him out closely? What was she doing?

Suddenly, a voice rung in his head. One that filled him with such a horror his heart almost stopped.

"A, B, C...It's easy as one, two, three..."

Then he screamed. Inside of the prison that was his own body, Mads started screaming with utter terror.

17

APRIL 2014

"So what do we do next?" Sune asked.

"We know the guy probably went to a murder party game or fundraiser at noon on the Saturday that Maya disappeared," I said. "Maya hit him with the car at two o'clock, not far from the theater." Rebekka had found a map of the town and we were now looking at how far away from the theater the accident took place. It was very close. "So, we must assume he was on his way home from this party? And that was when he stepped out in front of the car without looking. Right?"

The others nodded.

"So, I'm thinking it's a good idea to find out who else was at this party," I continued. "Maybe someone else left the party at the same time he did. Maybe they saw Maya...." I paused. It was really far-fetched. There was already a guy that had seen her drive off. Maybe it was about time I just admitted that she had run off? "No. It's no use," I said resigned.

"Why?" Rebekka asked. "I think it's a great idea. I mean, what harm can it do to check it out, huh? So what if we don't learn anything about where Maya is? At least we will have tried. It's better than just sitting here and waiting, right?"

I looked at her. She was a very pretty woman. And she was so right. I couldn't stand just sitting and waiting anymore. I needed to act. I needed to at least do something. I didn't feel like the police were doing anything at all to help me out. It was brutal to have to just wait for her to show up on her own.

"You're right," I said. "At least we're doing something here. Let's find these people. As far as I can see, twenty-two people other than Mads Schou were supposed to attend this party. I say we contact every one of them and ask about what went on and if they saw Mads leave."

"We'll say it's for an article," Rebekka said. "Sune can give Morten one of his cameras to make him look like a photographer. Tell them it's only research so far, no interviews yet. That'll make them talk. People say more if they're not held accountable afterwards. That's why people would rather speak to a journalist than the police. As long as you promise not to quote them for anything."

"Sounds like a plan to me," I said and looked at Morten.

Sune handed him one of his cameras.

"Anything for you," Morten said to me, as he took the camera.

I looked through the Facebook invitation and found the list of people who had stated that they would participate. "Look," I said and pointed at a name. "Signe Schou. That's his wife. She was also going to be there."

"Good," Rebekka said. "Why haven't we heard about her before? I didn't see her at the hospital."

"That's what I've been wondering about," I said. "I've been at the hospital to visit Mads every day since we got back and I haven't seen her once or heard them mention her name."

"That's a little strange, isn't it?" Morten asked.

"It's very strange," I said pensively. I scrolled through Signe Schou's profile to see if anything jumped out at me, but nothing really did. Only the fact that the last time she had updated her profile was on the day of the accident. At nine in the morning she had written the letters: YNWA on Mads' wall. Just like her husband had posted on hers the day before. Were they just very big soccer fans? Signe didn't appear to be according to her profile. There were no updates about Liverpool, or any other team, for that matter. She hadn't even put them under interests or groups and she hadn't liked their fan page. Why would she write something like this? Just because her husband was into this?

"So how do you suggest we go about this? There are no numbers or addresses of these people who were at the party. All we know are their names and their Facebook profiles."

I looked at Rebekka. I had a good feeling about this. I couldn't put my finger on it, but something about this direction we were about to take made sense. It simply felt right.

"I suggest we just write a message to these people one after another, explaining to them who we are, that we work for the newspaper and that we're doing a story about Mads and we're going to write about him, a nice portrait about the person he was before the accident and then wait for them to take the bait."

18

APRIL 2012

They got a suite at one of the many five-star resorts stretching along Alanya's silky sand beaches on the southern coast of Turkey. Mads and Signe soon visited all the attractions, sun-bathed during the day and partied well into the night. They took a Dolmuş to visit the Alanya castle and saw the Red tower on one day, on another they took a boat trip and saw all the caves, then they went scuba diving, and later on a Jeep Safari and even rode a donkey one day. They rented scooters or walked and soon they had seen everything. Signe had gotten a nice tan and was bored with lying on the beach, trying to sleep away her hangovers. Mads was getting more and more dull again and she was tired of the way he constantly jumped around and served her, like he was her little monkey. He made sure she had everything she needed and it annoyed her more than ever. They went shopping excessively to make Signe happy, but the joy didn't last long. Spending money like they didn't care was fun at first, but soon became dull. There were no more dresses she wanted to buy and no more shoes or souvenirs she desired. After a week and a half, Signe believed she had seen it all and she was starting to lose interest. In both the town and in him.

"So what do you want to do today?" Mads asked over breakfast.

A small part of the omelet was stuck in his beard as he spoke. He was beginning to look like a bush-man, Signe thought, and felt like shaving him, but even that thought bored her.

"I got another e-mail from my mom," Mads continued.

Signe didn't even bother to look at him. She scrolled her news feed on Facebook. No one at home seemed to be doing anything interesting either. It was still boringly cold in Denmark and they were—as usual—expecting spring to come right around the corner. One of her friends had posted a picture of her and her boyfriend sitting outside in their yard enjoying the sun wearing big winter jackets and beanies. That was Denmark in the spring for you, Signe thought to herself. Who needed that?

"What does she want?" Signe asked without caring about the answer.

"She's asking us when we're coming home. She found a house that she thinks will be perfect for us."

"She has now, has she?" Signe answered without interest.

"Yeah. So what do you want me to tell her?"

Signe shrugged and finished her coffee. "I don't know. Tell her we don't know. What do I care? She's your mother."

"Yes, but when are we coming home?" Mads asked. "We have to get back at some point. I'm supposed to start in my dad's firm as soon as we do. We should at least give them something to work with, don't you think we owe that to them?"

Signe looked at her husband. She hated that he always wanted to be so sensible. She didn't enjoy that side of him. She liked his adventurous side. She liked it when he went crazy with jealousy or with rage or passion. Oh, how she longed for passion, some sort of spark in him and in her life as well. Something to let her know that they were still alive and not just another dead couple, just waiting for life to be over.

She wanted more out of her time here on this boring earth.

"We don't owe them anything," she said with a grin.

"We are, after all, living off the money they gave us." Mads sighed and rubbed his forehead. "I don't know what we were thinking. I mean, it's been fun and all, but how are we going to explain it to my parents?"

Signe shrugged with a light grin. "We don't."

"Don't what?"

"Don't explain it," she said and took another bite of the sugary croissant that she had pushed into the middle of the table because she thought was done.

Mads wrinkled his forehead. Signe hated when he did that. It was something a father or an old teacher would do. It was so...bourgeois. So incredibly boring.

"I don't understand."

Of course you don't. It doesn't fit with your desperate need to please your parents, does it?

"Don't answer the e-mail, don't call them. Don't talk to them at all. Then you don't have to explain anything, see?"

Signe leaned forward and grabbed his hand in hers. "Let's see where life takes us. We can't go back. I don't want to go back to that boring old country and sit in some house from the eighties and spit out kids that will ruin my body and then bother me till I die. I want to live, Mads. I want to really live."

She paused and waited for him to fully understand what she was saying. She'd had this feeling ever since they were in that restroom in Egypt looking at the bartender lying on the tiles bleeding from his head. The adrenalin, the excitement, she needed it. She craved it. And she knew she could never get it back in boring old Denmark. Somehow, she sensed that she was never going home again. There was no way she could go back.

"But...but...our families?"

"What families? I only have my mother and I'm not missing her, to be honest. Think about it Mads. With what happened in Egypt, I don't think it is even smart for us to go back. They might come looking for us. It's better to lay low for a little while."

Mads nodded. He knew what she meant. He had worried about it too. Signe knew that and didn't feel guilty about using it to get her way. Signe was smiling. She could tell he was about to cave in now. She had him wrapped around her pinky.

"Okay. I guess I won't write back to her then," he said. He paused and looked at the screen of his iPad with the expensive alligator skin cover that his mother had bought him for his birthday. The cover alone was worth

more than four thousand dollars, Signe had seen on the Internet. If everything else went wrong, they could always sell that. That or her engagement
ring that had cost almost thirty thousand dollars.

"So, what do you want to do today?" Mads asked, slightly shaken with
the decision he had just made. He put the iPad down.

Signe looked up from her phone and their eyes met. She felt a tickling
sensation inside of her again. She never wanted it to go away.

"I think we should do something really fun, what do you say? Let's spike
things up a little. I have an idea."

19

APRIL 2014

"I'm glad you came this fast," the man said to the numerologist.

They were walking down the hallway with the many doors on each side all looking the same, except for the numbers changing from door to door.

"Of course," the numerologist said.

"She woke up only fifteen minutes ago. It's right in here." The man pointed at the white door with the number fifty-seven on it.

"Thank you," the numerologist said. "I'll take it from here."

The man nodded and backed away. The numerologist waited a few seconds till she was certain he was going away, then opened the door.

She was sitting on the bed. Her feet pulled close to her body. She looked like a very young girl. She turned her head and looked at the numcrologist when she entered. The numerologist smiled what seemed to be a friendly smile.

"Hi Zelllena."

The girl looked confused. "Who are you?" she asked. "Where am I?"

"I know you probably have a lot of questions, Zelllena and I will try and answer most of them."

"Zelllena?" the girl said. "Is that my name?"

"Yes. That is your name. You're here because we're trying to help you. You got yourself in trouble some days ago and we're trying to help you get better."

The girl looked troubled. "Why don't I remember anything?"

"You suffer from amnesia. But it's all for the best. This way, we can give you a fresh start. You need to let go of your past."

The numerologist felt so excited, but tried to tone it down. Being able to help Zelllena out and get a new life for her was just so giving of herself. It was the best feeling in the world.

"I feel so strange," Zelllena said. She looked out the window. The sky was gray and heavy clouds were building.

The numerologist knew it was going to take a while for her to accept her new life, but she would come around. She was going to enjoy it eventually.

"It's this month," the numerologist said. "It seems to be bothering most people these days. It's the planets and the numbers, you know? April is a big month. It is one of the most pivotal months of the whole entire year."

The girl seemed interested. "What do you mean?"

The numerologist smiled. She loved when people wanted to know more. Numerology and astronomy were her passion and she loved to talk about it and teach people how to improve their lives with very few changes. It was truly a blessing to have been given such an insight to this world and its energies.

"There is so much dynamic and vast energy in this month," she said and sat on the bed next to Zelllena. "We're in Aries in the start of the month, it's the first sign of the Zodiac and Aries is all about a fresh start and new beginnings. So that fits well for you, I think. Aries is, in general, the celebration of the self. But this year, Mars is currently in the sign of Libra and Libra is all about relationships and harmony, plus it is in retrograde, meaning that, from the earth's perspective, it looks like it's moving backwards. This means you have this strong forward moving planet that is now being feminine and moving backwards. Now, what does all that mean? Well, it means that every time we feel like we're moving forwards towards something, it can feel like we're taking some steps backwards. So I believe that what the universe is telling us this month is that, instead of moving forward with all of our goals and dreams, it wants us to pace ourselves and make sure that we have harmony and balance in our lives. And that is what I want for you to have Zelllena. You need a more balanced life. But this explains why you might feel a little frustrated right now. There is so much you want to do with your life, but you can't because life gets in your way. You certainly were frustrated and very angry before you came to me for help. You weren't feeling good. And this explains it. Plus we have to remember that 2014 is a seven universal year. Let's not forget that, right?"

The numerologist broke into laughter and poked Zelllena in the side with her elbow. The girl didn't laugh. She still looked confused, the poor thing.

"Seven is the number of the soul," the numerologist tried to explain, but the girl didn't seem to get that part either. She really didn't know anything, did she? "If you add the numbers two, zero, one and four you get seven, so that's how you calculate the number of the year. But we also have a lot of opposite planets this month and if you draw them, you get a square, and squares are all about tension. When you have a square, you can feel like you're being boxed in...a lot of pressure without an outlet. I've decided to help you release that pressure. But I want you to remember that April 2014 is an eleven universal month. Eleven is the number of intuition. It is also the number of light. It's all about bringing more light into your life. This eleven energy is going to bring light to all the dark places inside of you. The parts of you that haven't been given any attention will all be coming to the surface. So, what do you say? Are you excited?"

Zelllena looked at the numerologist for a long time. "I'm really very tired," she finally said. "Can I go to sleep now?"

The numerologist pursed her lips.

"I brought you something." The numerologist held up a small leather bag. Zelllena didn't seem interested, so she opened it herself.

"They are crystals. I'll place them all over your room. They'll protect you against anger and negative energies and make you feel better. I brought some for healing as well. They'll help you. Just wait and see."

Zelllena didn't even look at her as she placed the crystals around the room. It annoyed the numerologist. When she was done, she looked at the girl and sighed.

"Well, I guess I'm just going to have to be patient with you. But you'll get it. I am certain you will eventually. I'll keep you here until you do."

20

APRIL 2014

"I can't say I knew Mads very well."

The woman sitting in front of us smiled gently as she sat down. She was young, around nineteen or so. She lived in a small apartment in downtown Karrebaeksminde close to the newspaper's office.

Morten was with me. Our group had split up into teams. As soon as we had started messaging the people that were invited to the party on Facebook, a few of them had answered that they would be happy to help. Rebekka and Sune had gone to see a guy who told us he knew Mads pretty well, while Morten and I had gone to visit this young woman by the name of Sascha DuBois. She seemed to be slightly confused when we arrived, but as soon as we sat on the very colorful couch in her living room, she seemed to calm down. She served us a cup of coffee.

"That's okay," I said and took out my pencil and notepad. "We'll be talking to many people, so your contribution to the article will probably be very small. But anything you can tell us about him and the party you were attending when he was hit by the car would be great."

"What you really should do is to talk to Bettina Nielsen. She was the one flirting with Mads at the party."

I nodded and made a note of it for later. "We definitely will. She was one of the people that responded to our message as well. You said she flirted with him? What about his wife, wasn't she there as well?"

"She never showed up," Sascha said. "Rumors have it the two of them had split up and were living separately. They were married only two years ago, you know. Everyone thought they were way too young, but they didn't care. Not even when Mads' mother tried to stop them. Did you know she tried to pay off Signe to not marry Mads?"

"No, we did not," I said.

"Well, don't put it in the paper or anything, but she did. She offered her a huge check, but apparently Signe's mother didn't think it was enough. She wanted more money for her daughter and the only way to get that was to marry the guy. That's what the rumors say anyway. It's all very strange with that family."

I wrote on my pad that the mother had tried to pay the wife off. I couldn't stop wondering where this wife, this Signe Schou was now and why she hadn't been at the hospital to visit her husband? Had the mother told her to stay away? She must have heard about it by now. Wasn't she allowed to at least say goodbye? I felt bad for the girl.

"So, could you please explain to us exactly what happened at the party? You were all invited through Facebook, right?" I asked.

"Yes. We received an invitation just three days before, which I thought was odd since most people are busy and can't all of a sudden take out an entire day to go to a party. But it was also intriguing. I had never been to a murder party before and I had never been to a party that started in the middle of the day. I had to go. I had to see what it was."

"And, what was it?" Morten asked.

"I arrived at the old theater at noon. The front door was open, so I walked right in. I remember feeling very excited. As I walked into the big lobby where the party was held, I saw a few familiar faces and then a lot I didn't know."

"Was Mads Schou there when you arrived?"

"Yes. He was standing at the bar with a drink, flirting with that Bettina person. I always had a thing for Mads, you know, so I felt a slight pinch of jealousy. Well, I guess we all had something for him back in high-school.

He was the handsome rich guy. I just never really cared much for Bettina, so I guess that's why it annoyed me so much. I mean, I know the guy's married, but I'd heard the rumors that they were having trouble."

I nodded and noted it on my pad. The married couple was having trouble, I wrote.

"So, Bettina Nielsen was talking to him and then what happened?" I asked.

"I talked to some guy for a little while waiting for the party to begin. I remember we discussed what was going to happen. None of us had been to a party like this before. There were free drinks, so we had a couple of shots to get us going, then a cocktail or two. Still, nothing happened and I was beginning to think nothing ever would. That it was just another dull party, but soon something did."

"What happened?" I asked and looked into the girl's eyes.

"The lights went out."

"Then what happened?"

"Then someone screamed."

21

APRIL 2014

"Was it like a fake scream? Like they were having fun, playing a game, or what?" Morten asked.

"I thought so at first, but then I realized it wasn't. Soon others started screaming and panic spread in the darkness. I tried to walk towards the door, but when I got there, it was locked. I couldn't see anything. There were no windows."

"Why haven't you told the police all this?" Morten asked. "They don't even know about the party, do they? Or that Mads was there?"

Sascha shrugged. "I didn't think it mattered. He was hit by the car in the street when he left the party. It had nothing to do with us."

"Back to the party," I interrupted. "Everybody was now screaming and trying to get out of the doors, right?"

"Right. But they were locked."

"What happened next?" I asked.

"Well, that's the strangest part. I thought it was all part of the game. I kept waiting for the lights to go back on and the game to begin. You know, someone lying on the floor pretending to be dead and then we had to figure out who among us did it. But the lights never came on. Instead, there was a thud and another scream. I heard voices in the darkness and then people fighting. People were screaming and whimpering and wondering whether it was part of the game or not. I was standing close to the door when suddenly it was kicked open and people started storming out. Light came into the room from the outside, but I never saw what had been going on in the room, since people left in such a hurry. It was really a disaster. Not very well planned."

"So, did you see when Mads left?"

"I suppose he was running just like the rest of them. I didn't see him in the crowd. That hall was emptied pretty fast and people scattered."

"So, no one was hurt? Why were they screaming then?" I asked.

"I have no idea. Maybe it was just all a joke. I really don't know," Sascha said.

"You said there were voices," I asked. "What did they say? Could you hear what they were talking about?"

"They seemed to be arguing about something. There were a lot of different sounds and people screaming. But they sounded like they were arguing."

"Do you remember anything they said?"

Sascha shook her head. "Not really. Yes, there was something that I'm pretty sure was said. It was the number eleven and something about it being able to bring light in the darkness." Sascha looked like she didn't really believe it. She shook her head. "I don't know. Maybe I heard wrong. It might have been something else."

It didn't sound like anything we could use, but I wrote it down anyway. I felt frustrated as I looked at my notes. I wasn't getting any closer to my daughter with this. It was all very strange and didn't seem to have anything to do with the accident. But at least now I knew why Mads might have been running from the theater and into the street. He might have been scared in the darkness and, just like the rest of the party, he ran as soon as the door was opened. Maybe there really wasn't much here for me to discover. Someone played a prank on these people that caused them to run. Mads was just unlucky enough to run straight into my daughter's car.

"Just to clarify," I said. "You didn't see Mads run out into the street and get hit by the car?"

"No. As far as I know, it happened behind the theater. I ran the other way. I wanted to go home and I live in the opposite direction."

"So you never saw the car that hit him or what happened afterwards?" I asked, still hoping for anything that could help me out.

Sascha shook her head. "Good gosh no. I would have told the police if I did, now wouldn't I?"

"Of course you would," I said, disappointed. I looked at Morten. "Well, I guess we have what we came for."

I got up from the couch. Morten followed. In the doorway, I turned to face Sascha. "Thank you so much for taking the time to talk to us."

"No problem. I hope you have enough. As I told you, I don't know Mads very well. I mostly remember him from high school, but I don't think he ever noticed me."

"Say, do you have any idea who invited all of you to this party?" Morten suddenly asked.

I took over. "We've been wondering about it. On the Facebook invitation, it just says that it is the club called *Mystery-murder club* that created the event. That was also the name that was given to the theater when the person rented the premises for the party. It was paid in cash sent by mail, they told us when we called. On Facebook, the club has no members yet, but the moderator of it is someone calling himself M. Arple. There are no photos on his—or her—profile or any other information."

Sascha bit her lip and shook her head. "No, I can't say that I do. I wondered who was behind it as well, but figured they wanted to be anonymous to make it more fun. It was kind of the premise of the entire thing. It had to be all secretive, right? It had to be a mystery to get people's attention to get them to come."

22

APRIL 2012

B eing blonde and visiting Turkey had become quite annoying for Signe. The many stares from men she met in the streets had been enjoyable in the beginning, but after a couple of days, it had become unbearable. She could hardly walk into a shop without the owner asking to touch her hair and giving her unwanted attention. Even just walking in the streets of Alanya, she was constantly stopped by people, especially old women reaching their hands out to touch her hair like it was somehow magical or especially blessed. At the hotel, they had told her to be careful and not to go out alone and never to wander into dark and deserted streets.

Now that they were leaving the hotel at night, she had put on a scarf to cover her hair. She was wearing a long coat covering most of her body and holding her husband's hand as they walked into the heavily lit street.

"Now, will you tell me where we're going?" Mads asked. He didn't feel comfortable not knowing what she was up to. Not after what happened in Egypt.

Signe had been very secretive all day while preparing what she had planned. She had been to a shop downtown all alone in the afternoon but never showed what she bought to Mads. She had gotten dressed in the bathroom and put on make-up, brushed her short blonde hair carefully, then covered it all up with a scarf and the long black coat.

"Not yet," she said with a grin. "It's a surprise."

Mads was tipsy and it affected his sense of judgment. He was intrigued, but at the same time, very scared of what she might have come up with. The alcohol sedated his strength and capability of saying no to Signe.

They had been drinking in the hotel room. They had ordered wine and champagne through room service, then emptied the many small vodka bottles in the mini-bar. Signe was drunk too. She looked at Mads and he felt a chill go through his body, a thrill of excitement. She looked so happy. He liked that. But it also made him feel anxious.

"Just tell me," he said with a slightly shivering voice.

"In time, my dear. In time," she said, as they turned a corner and walked into a smaller street. The streetlights were gone and suddenly it was darker.

"Are you sure this is the way?" he asked. "It doesn't look safe to go down this street."

"I know," Signe said. "We'll be fine. Just trust me."

She took another turn around a corner and brought them into an even darker street. "It should be around here somewhere," she said.

"What should?" he asked.

They weren't alone in the streets anymore. In every doorway they spotted figures, mostly women in short dresses. Eyes followed their every move from every building.

"I'm not sure I feel comfortable here," Mads said.

"Don't be so dull," Signe said and pulled his arm.

Dark faces stared at them from corners and doorways. Dogs barked. The distant sound of music came from somewhere. Lights coming from the windows were dampened by heavy red curtains. Signe took one last turn into an alley with no outlet. Then she stopped.

"This is it," she whispered her voice trembling with excitement. "This is just perfect."

"This place?" Mads asked with horror in his voice. "What is it? Why are we here? Signe I really think we should be getting back."

They weren't alone in the alley, they soon realized. From the corners and doorways on the sides, there were movements...there were people. Dark faces on well-built bodies were approaching them slowly.

Mads froze. This place scared him. "Let's get out of here, Signe. Come. Let's go dancing at that club we went to last night. You had fun there, remember?"

"No. We've been to every club in town. It's all just for the tourists. I want to experience the real Turkey...the raw and dangerous side to this country. Not just the plastic part made neat for us tourists, no...the dirty and disgusting part. The part that is hidden."

"But...Signe. You know it isn't safe. The hotel owner specifically told us to stay far away from areas like this! Don't you remember? He told us to remember that Turkish men didn't have same respect for women as they do in Europe. That a blonde girl like you could easily get herself into trouble. These are not people you should mess with. Don't you remember the case of the nine year old Norwegian girl who was raped here?"

Signe smiled as the men came closer. Mads didn't understand what she was up to. What was the idea with this? What was her plan? Then she threw her head back and took off the scarf to let her blonde hair fall down. She grabbed her coat and pulled it open, revealing her body dressed in nothing but a very small tight black mini dress with front openings showing her voluptuous breasts very clearly. Signe threw the coat at Mads, then moaned in enjoyment as the men approached her like wolves approaching prey.

"Signe, please listen to me," Mads pleaded anxiously. He couldn't believe his eyes. What the hell what she doing? "We need to leave now. You don't realize what you're doing. You're drunk."

But Signe didn't answer. Five men were now circling her, one pushed Mads to the side. Another grabbed Signe by the hair and pulled her close to him.

"You wanna fuck, bad boy?" Signe asked.

The nasty man smiled. "Yes. We fuck you little girl. We fuck you so bad you never walk again."

Mads shrieked as another man grabbed Signe from behind and made her bend forward, then grabbed her dress and pulled it up. Another man slammed his fist into her face and she fell to the ground with a scream. Mads felt so helpless. These men were so much bigger than he. Why would Signe do this to herself? To them? Why? There was no way Mads could save her this time.

"Little bitch," one of the men said, then pulled his pants down. "Now, you suck."

The man who had hit her in her face grabbed her by the hair and pulled her up towards his crotch. Someone was behind her, trying to climb her. Mads started screaming.

"HELP! Someone help us, please?"

As the man in front of her tried to stuff his thing into her mouth, Signe opened her mouth and then screamed.

"Now Mads! The coat! Check the pocket!"

The pocket?

Frantically, Mads grabbed the coat and pulled out a gun. He gasped when he saw it. Signe was screaming loudly now. The men were all over her, hitting her, and trying to rape her.

"Do it, Mads!" she screamed. "Kill them! Save me!"

Mads was sweating heavily, still staring at the weapon he was holding in his hand. He had shot rifles many times on his parent's estate. They went hunting every year on the first day of October, riding their horses, and he had shot everything from deer to foxes. But he had never shot people.

Signe was screaming loudly now. They were really hurting her. Mads lifted the gun. He was shaking and had to use both hands to hold it still. He opened his mouth and let out a terrifying scream, then pulled the trigger. One after another, they fell to the ground. Mads shot the men right in the heart, the way his father had taught him to shoot wild animals as a child.

"Get off of her, you motherfuckers!" he roared.

Seconds later, they were all on the ground. Blood was gushing from their wounds. One was still moving in spasms. Mads stood over him, then shot him in the face while screaming his rage and furor out.

Signe was still lying on the ground, moaning in pain from all the punches. Mads ran to her and picked her up. Her face was swollen and red.

The area around her right eye was already swollen to twice its usual size. Signe was crying. Then laughing, then crying again.

Mads kneeled next to her and picked her up. He carried Signe over his shoulder all the way back to the hotel.

In their room at the resort, he put ice on her bruises and held her hand while she fell asleep. Meanwhile, in his quiet mind, he promised himself that tomorrow morning he would leave her. Tomorrow, he would do it.

Tomorrow.

23

APRIL 2014

Bettina Nielsen greeted us in the doorway of a small house outside of town flanked by her three big German Shepherds. She was about the same age as Sascha, only nineteen and worked at the hospital as a porter to make money enough to travel, she told us, when we were shown into the kitchen.

"I want to see the world before I start studying," she said and fed one of the dogs a treat. "I'm travelling through Asia with my backpack this summer. That's why I still live with my parents. It's easier to save up money this way."

I sat down on a kitchen chair and Bettina offered us coffee. We accepted.

"A lot of kids did that too, when I was your age," I said, thinking about my own years after high school. They hadn't exactly turned out the way I had wanted them to. Getting pregnant all of a sudden hadn't exactly been part of my dreams for my life after high school. I had wanted to travel as well, like most of my classmates did. I had wanted to just live the easy life of a backpacker through Thailand, India and Bali. But that hadn't been in the cards for me.

"The way I figure, it's now or never, right? I mean, before I marry and the kids come along and I'm unable to do anything," Bettina said.

"Well you're not exactly unable to do anything," I said. "It's just something different."

"Yeah, I'm not really looking forward to that. All the diapers and the lack of sleep. It's not really me. Not yet that is. Maybe I'll change my mind. My older sister never did. She never had children and she's past thirty now. I don't know what's best. To live alone as a pathetic thirty-year old and still go to parties like you're nineteen or to have children destroy your life. I know I don't want to be anything like my sister, so maybe I'll change my mind."

"Most women do," I said, while looking through my notes from our visit at Sascha's.

Bettina served us some coffee and Danish butter cookies, then sat down at the table next to us. "I hope they're not too old," she said as she put the plate of cookies in front of me. "I don't know when my mom bought them."

"I'm sure they're fine," I said and grabbed one. I tasted it. "They're good," I said with a smile.

"Great," Bettina said. "I never touch those things. Too much sugar, you know."

I forced an awkward smile and stared at the skinny girl. "Well, you're missing out," I said and grabbed another one, just to show her I wasn't going to let her comment get to me.

"So, you wanted to talk to me about Mads Schou?" she asked. "I'm surprised you came to me, since I really don't know him that well. We both went to the same high school, but he was two years older than me, so I hardly think he knew who I was. I've never really spoken to him."

"That's funny," I said and looked at her to see if I could tell if she was lying to me. "Because we spoke to Sascha DuBois earlier today and she told us you were talking to Mads Schou at the party on the day he was hit by the car."

"She did what?" Bettina asked.

"As a matter of fact, she told us you were flirting with him," Morten said in the tone of a police officer. "Is that true?"

"No! Absolutely not," Bettina said. "She said that? That little...conniving...I can't believe she would..."

"So, you're telling us she's lying?" I asked. I sipped my coffee and decided not to have another cookie. They did taste a little old.

"Yes, she's lying. I never spoke to the man. She was the one who always had a thing for him. She always talked about him at school, about how rich he was and how gorgeous he was. Constantly blabbering on and on about him. And he was single throughout all of high school, so she thought she might have a chance and spoke with him at every party. But he never showed any interest in her. And suddenly rumors said he had found this other girl. She was from another school, I believe. Quite the troublemaker who had been thrown out of several schools over the years. She never finished high school, as far as I know. He ended up marrying her like less than a year after he graduated. It was quite the story around here, since everybody believed he only married her because she was pregnant."

I almost spat out my coffee. "She was pregnant?"

Bettina shrugged. "Yes. He knocked her up and had to marry her, but later it turned out she wasn't pregnant after all."

"She lost it?" I asked.

"Well, no one really knows what happened. Rumors say she made it up to get him to marry her. Actually, the story goes it was her mother who made her do it. After what I heard, Mads' mother tried to pay off Signe to not date her son anymore and then Signe's mother decided to go for the big bucks, if you know what I mean. She smelled a way for her daughter to get out of the slums and, since Signe couldn't stay in a school long enough to get an education, this was a way for her to be secure. Marry the guy and live the rich life. Maybe divorce him later and run away with half of the money."

"Wow, that's cynical," I said.

"Right? I can't believe anyone can think like that. But, as I said, it's all just rumors. I don't know if it's true or not. But I guess they say there is always a grain of truth to a rumor, huh? But people did say that Mads really loved her. That he would do anything for her. I don't know if she ever loved him. I don't know if she is even capable of loving anyone. She is one messed up kid."

"How do you know?" I asked.

"Well most people know what happened to her in her childhood. Her dad was arrested for pedophilia when she was nine years old. God only knows what he did to her before it was discovered. The story was in the newspapers and everything. Apparently, he was a kindergarten teacher and had groped and touched a lot of children in class, trying to make them believe it was natural and normal. They found tons of child-porn on his computer and, when they interviewed Signe, she talked about sex like it was an everyday thing and she wasn't a virgin anymore. Everybody in town felt so sorry for the girl."

I felt appalled and slightly nauseated. This didn't seem to have anything to do with Maya's disappearance, but it still interested me. I had a hard time understanding these kinds of things. How you can hurt your own child like that. I missed Maya again and hoped that she was somewhere safe. A big part of me had started to wish that she had just run off and was hiding somewhere till the storm blew over, but in my heart I knew that wasn't the truth.

"So you say that Sascha was lying when she told us you were flirting with Mads Schou at the party. How do you know? Couldn't she just have seen you standing close to each other ordering a drink or something?" Morten asked.

"No. I know she's lying because she was the one talking to him. She was in the bar talking to him, flirting with him until the lights went out. We talked briefly at the party and she told me she had heard that Mads and Signe were having trouble and that she was going to try and make a move on him. She was very happy to see that Signe wasn't there and took it as a sign to move in on him. I told her it was probably too early, since everyone knew how much he loved Signe, but Sascha was certain it was the right time. I even saw her follow him outside as soon as the doors were opened and everyone ran out.

I stopped and looked up from my notepad. "She did what?"

"When I got outside, I saw Mads run behind the building like he was running for his life and I saw Sascha run after him."

24

APRIL 2014

W e thanked Bettina for her time, then drove back to Sascha's apartment and knocked on the door. She looked very surprised when she saw us.

"Did you forget something?" she asked.

"You lied to us," I said. "We talked to Bettina."

Sascha's smile froze. Her face went red. "Don't believe anything she says. She is a liar."

"Don't give me that," I said. "Can we come in?"

"I don't owe you anything. It's not like you're the police or anything."

Morten held his badge in the air. "As a matter of fact, I am," he said. "Please let us come in and hear your side of the story. The truth this time."

Sascha looked like she was weighing her options. Then she bowed her head and opened the door to let us inside. She sat with her hands in her lap and didn't look at us as she spoke.

"Okay, so I was the one who talked with Mads at the party until like ten minutes before the lights were turned out. I had to use the restroom and left him. Once I got back into the lobby, everything went dark. I didn't see him again until I spotted him outside."

"Why did you lie?" I asked.

Sascha shrugged. "I guess I didn't like to admit I was defeated. Mads showed no interest in me whatsoever."

"I don't think that was it," I said. "I think there's something else. Something you're hiding from us. You saw something, didn't you?"

Sascha shook her head. "No. No. I didn't. I spoke to him for a little while, then he lost interest."

I sighed and leaned back on her couch. I couldn't believe she would continue to lie to us. "Come on, Sascha," I said. "Tell us the truth. We know you ran after him when you got outside. It's important to us."

Sascha closed her eyes for a short while. I gave her a second to gather her thoughts. When she opened her eyes, they were moist.

I gasped. "You saw what happened to Mads, didn't you?"

A tear left the corner of her eye and rolled across her cheek. She wiped it away. "It was awful. I...I haven't told anyone."

"Why didn't you tell the police?"

"Because I was afraid she would come after me next," she said. "She saw me standing there. She knew I saw what happened."

"Whoa. Let's go back a little," I said. "Who saw you? There was someone else there?"

Sascha nodded. Morten found a paper towel for her to wipe her face. She was crying more now.

"Who was she?" I asked.

"I don't know. She was just suddenly there. I hadn't seen her. Everything was so chaotic. People were running outside. I was close to the door, so I was one of the first ones out. When I got out of the theater, I was looking to see if I could find Mads and I spotted him running around the back, then decided to follow after him. Maybe we could split a taxi, I thought. Maybe I could buy myself a little extra time in his company, let him get to know me better, maybe ask if he wanted to go out for a drink one day. I don't know what I was thinking, but I followed him around the building and towards the street. He was running really fast and I couldn't catch up with him, so eventually, I slowed down and realized I would never talk to him again. That was when I saw her. She appeared out of the blue. She was running up right behind him. I don't think he saw her until it was too late. Then she did it. She pushed him into the street where he was hit by the car. It all happened really fast. I had no idea what to do. I saw him lying on the asphalt and the woman standing still on the sidewalk staring at him like she enjoyed watching him in pain. That was when I decided to run back. I was terrified. If that woman was capable of pushing Mads like that, then she wouldn't hesitate before doing the same to me if she knew I had seen it. I was certain she would want to kill me."

"So you ran back and kept quiet?" Morten asked.

"Yes. I'm, not proud of it, but that was what I decided to do. I was so scared. I never saw who she was, though. She was wearing a blue shirt and black pants. She had her red hair in a ponytail. That's all I remember. I only saw her from behind. All I noticed was that she seemed tall. That's all."

"The car," I said frantically. Finally, some light was shed onto what had happened. "Did you see what happened to the girl who was driving the car?"

Sascha shook her head. "No. I didn't even see her at all. I've read about her in the papers and all, but I didn't look at her at all. I only looked at Mads. I was certain he was dead. It was a pretty hard hit. I can still hear the sound of the car hitting his body when I'm lying in my bed at night. I dream about the hit constantly, about him being thrown into the air and then that awful sound of him hitting the asphalt afterwards. Makes me shiver just thinking about it."

"You have to go to the police with this," Morten said. "They need to know."

Sascha nodded with a bowed head. "Of course. I guess I knew I was going to have to eventually. I just hoped it wouldn't be necessary. I hoped they would figure it out on their own, but they haven't, have they?"

"No," Morten said.

I left Sascha's apartment with a strange feeling inside. I was happy that I had gotten a step closer to what happened to Maya and now I could finally say that she had been telling the truth when I spoke to her. She didn't stand a chance. The guy was pushed into the road in front of her. She couldn't have stopped. But I still didn't know what happened to her next. I had an awful feeling that woman had something to do with her disappearance. But who was she? And more importantly. Where was she?

25

APRIL 2014

The numerologist was hopping on one leg in the street while counting. "Three, five, seven..."

She could only step on every second tile; her foot could only touch the uneven numbers or she was afraid the entire mission would be jeopardized. The planets had been acting strangely this morning and she knew it was going to cause her trouble.

On her way to the girl's apartment, she caressed her rat in her pocket and spoke positive words to herself.

"You're independent. You're fun to be with. You're a three, you're a three. You're charismatic and popular. You have a rich inner life. You have balance."

On her way up the stairs, she passed a man and a woman on their way down. The numerologist smiled and told them to have a great day, then continued up to the door and knocked.

It hadn't taken her long to find the girl's address, but it wasn't until now that she had decided she needed to do something about her. She had seen what happened and she couldn't have her telling the police.

The door was opened and the girl's face appeared. "Yes?"

"Hello, dearie," the numerologist said. "Do you have any idea what your number for the day is?"

"Excuse me?" she said, looking confused.

The numerologist giggled. "Your number for the day. If you don't know it, I can give it to you. It can help you with your spirit and your energy today."

"No, I'm not interested. I'm not into anything like that, the girl said. She tried to close the door, but the numerologist put her hand on the door and blocked it. "Not so fast, dearie. I'm here to help you."

"I don't need any help. I'm...I was actually in the middle of something important. I don't have time for this. So, if you could please remove your hand from my door..."

"I can tell you that your number of the day is three! Well, aren't you lucky? That means you may feel as if an important change is taking place within, but are not yet clear about its true nature. You are going through a transforming growth spurt, and may not have much patience with yourself. Don't try to analyze what's going on, just roll with it," the numerologist said with a grin.

The girl looked perplexed. Like she thought the numerologist had lost her mind. "Are you trying to sell something? What do you want? I really don't have time for this..."

The numerologist gave the door a forceful push, causing the door to open so fast the girl couldn't react and it slammed right into her face. The girl fell backwards into the apartment, where she landed on the floor. The numerologist walked inside and slammed the door behind her.

"What the hell are you doing?" the girl hissed and tried to get up. The numerologist could hear the anxiety in the tone of her voice.

"I told you, dearie. I'm helping you."

The girl tried to crabwalk backwards on her arms. "Who are you? What is that? Is your pocket...moving?"

"Oh that. Well, yes. That's my friend Misty. I like to have her with me on days when Saturn is in retrograde. Well, that isn't exactly today, but I brought her anyway. Silly me, huh?" The numerologist laughed. "I guess I just like to have her with me when I feel lonely. She keeps me company."

"You're crazy," the girl said, still trying to get away. "I want you to leave my apartment immediately."

The numerologist tilted her head. "Ah, so sorry. No can do."

The girl moaned. Fear had struck her spirit and her eyes flamed in anxiety. "What do you want from me?"

"I don't want anything from you, my dear. I want you."

The girl shook her head fast. "No. No. Don't hurt me."

The numerologist pulled out a syringe from her pocket and stuck it into the girl's leg so fast the girl didn't manage to react.

"Oops," the numerologist said. "Guess it's too late."

26

APRIL 2012

Signe didn't leave the bed for two days. Mads gave her time to rest and made sure she had enough water and food. He fed her soup with a spoon because her lips and jaw were so badly bruised that she couldn't eat properly. Her arm was hurting badly too and Mads kept asking if she wanted him to take her to the hospital to check if it was broken. But Signe refused to go. She told him she just needed some rest.

"You were my hero," she said on the second day, when he helped her drink through a straw. "You saved me. I knew you would."

Mads sounded choked when he spoke. He hadn't said a word to her in two days and she knew he had been wondering what to do. In her short awake hours, she had worried that he would leave her, but he hadn't. Not yet, at least.

"Why did you do it?" he asked. "Why did you drag us out there and get yourself hurt like that? We could both have been killed. Why do you do these destructive things?"

She turned her eyes away. "I...I...didn't you like it? Didn't you have fun? You killed those people, Mads. Shot them dead one after another like this... paw...paw...paw," she said and pretended to be pointing at someone with a gun. "Didn't it feel great to save your wife like that?"

Mads made a frown. "No. No it didn't."

She didn't understand. How could he not have enjoyed that? She thought it was fun...exciting...electrifying. They were like freaking Bonnie and Clyde together.

"I thought you enjoyed it," she said. "Like killing that bartender. I wanted us to experience the same thrill as we had back then. I wanted us to feel alive. Don't you feel alive, Mads?"

He hid his face in his hands. When he looked at her again, he had been crying. Signe didn't enjoy seeing him like this. All red-eyed and weak. "Ah, come on, don't be a baby," she said, just like her dad had always told her when she had been red-eyed and sobbing after he was done with her. "You know you like it. You just don't want to admit it."

"No, I don't, Signe. I really didn't enjoy killing those people."

"Ah, come on. Don't be like that."

"Be like what? I'm only being sane here."

"Yes, yes, you're a true saint, aren't you? Can you honestly tell me you didn't feel any thrill, any small feeling of satisfaction for giving those bastards what they asked for?"

Mads went quiet. He scratched his beard. His silence was a good sign. That meant he had felt it. The question was whether he would admit it.

Just like you liked it when your dad touched you. Just like you knew deep down inside you enjoyed it, even when it hurt, you liked it. And he knew it. He knew you were nothing but a little whore. He was the only one who saw it.

"But we killed people, Signe. I shot them. They were all dead. How am I supposed to live with that? I killed that bartender in the restroom too. I'm not a murderer. I don't want to end my life in a Turkish prison."

"They were criminals, Mads. Part of the Turkish underworld. The police are going to thank us if they ever find out. No one is going to miss them. No one cares what happened to them."

"I do. I care. I'm the one who has to live with the fact that I've killed them. I'm the one who has to live with myself. Don't you understand that?"

She stared at him indifferently.

"I guess you don't," he said. "But this is the end of this, you hear me? If you ever pull a stunt like this again I will leave you. I will divorce you. I cannot do this again. I cannot play your little games anymore."

Mads sighed and stood up. He walked to the balcony and lit up a cigarette. Signe hadn't seen him smoke since before they were married. She liked it. Made him look like the bad boy she knew he was deep inside. The bad boy she was going to force out, whether he wanted to or not. The bad boy she wanted to be her husband and take over for that wimp that his mother had made him into. Yes, Signe was going to shape her husband into a man she could desire. No matter the cost. And they were never ever going to live in a small suburban house in Denmark, no matter how much he begged her. No matter how much his mother threatened them. Signe was in charge now and Mads was going to learn to like it.

27

APRIL 2014

We met with Rebekka and Sune back at the newspaper's office in the middle of town. Rebekka and Sune had both been back for a while when Morten and I entered.

"Hey guys," Sune said. He was eating something. Rebekka was too. I looked at the clock; it was past noon. No wonder I was hungry.

"We bought Smoerrebroed," Rebekka said. "The best from a place down at the harbor. There's enough for everybody. Just dig in."

I went to the small kitchen and grabbed two plates. I handed one to Morten, who found some sodas for us to drink. I grabbed a piece called a "shooting star." A piece of breaded fish on rye bread with shrimps, remoulade, dill and lemon on top. It was among my favorites.

We told them about our discovery while we ate. About how we had first spoken to Sascha, then Bettina and then gone back to Sascha to get the truth.

"So that means your daughter wasn't at fault," Rebekka said. "That's at least something."

"It is," I said with my mouth full. It was true that it soothed me a little to know that, but I felt anxious at the thought of the strange woman who had pushed Mads Schou out in front of the car. Where was she now? What had she done afterwards? If Sascha was afraid of her harming her, then could she have done something to Maya?

"It also means we're dealing with a murder case here," Morten said. "As soon as Sascha tells her story to the police, they'll go into the case with a brand new perspective, which can turn out to our advantage."

We all ate in silence for a few seconds. Then Rebekka spoke.

"So I bet you're afraid that this woman hurt Maya as well, huh?"

I closed my eyes. I really didn't want to think about it, but yes, she was spot on. That was exactly what I was afraid of. Could she have killed her and driven off with her body and dumped it somewhere? After all, Maya probably saw too much, or at least that could be what the woman thought. Maya hadn't mentioned anything about a woman on the phone, so my guess was that she hadn't seen her until she got out of the car. But the woman probably thought she had.

I felt Rebekka's hand on top of mine. She squeezed it gently. "I'm sure she's alright," she said.

I nodded and looked at her. I was beginning to like this Rebekka a lot. She seemed to truly care about this, about my story and not just because she wanted to sell newspapers.

"I have to believe she is. I can't lose hope, I simply can't," I said and drank from my orange soda.

"I understand," Rebekka said. "More than you know. Now let's tell them what we got out of our interviews."

Rebekka looked at Sune like she wanted him to begin. "Well, we went to see two people who were also at the party or reception or whatever you want to call it. The first one..."

"Stephen Pars," Rebekka interrupted him.

"Stephen Pars, yes," Sune continued. "A man a lot older than the two young girls you saw today. What was he?" Sune looked at Rebekka for the answer. "Thirty?"

"Twenty-nine," she corrected him. I loved the way the two of them were constantly supplementing each other. They knew each other well, I sensed. They just had a child together and also had one each from other relationships. It was great to see how well this kind of relationship could turn out. It gave me hope for me and Morten. It was always difficult when there were children involved.

"Yes, twenty-nine. Single, just gotten out of a long term relationship. Stephen saw the invite on Facebook and was curious. He thought that even if the party was dull and in the middle of the day, then there was still a possibility that he would be able to pick up a girl. So he decided to attend."

"The rest of his story resembles what yours told you," Rebekka took over while the two of them exchanged a secretive and caring look. I felt a sting of jealousy. Morten never looked at me the way Sune looked at Rebekka.

"You know, with the lights going out and people screaming and then all of them running outside."

"But there was one thing that he saw that I don't believe has been mentioned yet," Sune said.

"And what is that?" I asked.

"He said it was Mads who kicked the door open. He told us he didn't know Mads Schou before the party, but he had been standing next to him in the bar when the lights went out. They had talked about it for a second, you know, exchanged a couple of words wondering if the game had finally started. But then something happened to Mads, he said. He went quiet all of a sudden and then there was someone who whispered in the darkness. What was it that was said, Rebekka?"

"Someone whispered: *Easy as One, two, three.* Then Stephen heard Mads gasp and whimper and soon the voice started whispering numbers, telling him that his number of the day was four and that it meant that it was…," Rebekka looked into her notes and read out loud:

"*…a demanding day that will require plenty of focus, but ultimately, it furthers your overall progress. Be careful not to make promises you can't keep.*"

"That sounds strange," I said. "Can I see?"

Rebekka showed me what she had written on her pad. It was impossible to read her handwriting, so I accepted her word for it.

"He was very specific and remembered every word of it," Sune said. "I don't think anyone would lie about something like this."

"Well, you'd be surprised what people will lie about," Morten said. "I've seen stranger things than this."

"And what happened to Mads next?" I asked.

"Well, Stephen was certain someone was whispering this into Mads' ear and soon went quiet...maybe to await his response. Stephen believes that the same someone who had whispered also tried to hurt him. Mads was afraid of her, that was certain. He could hear him breathing heavily. Then he told her to leave him alone. She answered, '*no can do, sorry.*'"

"It was a her?" I asked, thinking about what Sascha DuBois had told me earlier in the day. "Is he certain of that?"

"Positive," Rebekka said.

"You said she tried to hurt him?" Morten asked. "How?"

"Stephen didn't know exactly, but it sounded like they were fighting in the darkness, and then Mads screamed like he was in pain. Somehow, he must have been able to get away from this person and run to the door and kick it open, because Stephen saw him as soon as the door opened and light entered...before everybody stormed out. It was Mads who kicked it open, but he had been hurt," Rebekka explained.

"How did he know that?" I asked.

Rebekka cleared her throat. "He was limping, Stephen told us. He was limping and holding a hand to his right thigh. Stephen was one of the few who stayed back when everyone else sprang for the door in panic. He wanted to see who had been fighting Mads, but there were too many people to see properly if someone was following him. But when the light from the outside hit the counter in the bar, Stephen saw a few drops of blood had dripped onto the floor underneath the stool where Mads had been sitting. He figured someone might have stabbed Mads in the leg before he ran."

"Let's check it out," I said and grabbed my jacket. I looked at Morten. "Are you coming?"

"Sure," he said and got up.

"Where are you going?" asked Rebekka.

"To the hospital."

28

APRIL 2014

They had been taking more tests all morning, but still hadn't found a match. Mads was happy to realize it was harder to find a match for his organs than anticipated, due to his rare blood type. All morning, he had been moving the tip of his pinky frantically hoping that someone would see it, but still he had no such luck. He was starting to wonder if they were even looking for signs that his brain was working anymore or not. Maybe it was simply that once the doctor had declared a patient brain-dead, then everyone stopped looking for him not to be, they simply gave up all hope.

Now he listened in as two nurses were checking his monitors as usual and changing his IV fluid bags. They were chatting about their husbands and the talking made Mads feel at ease. He had become terrified of being left alone. The loneliness of being trapped inside of his own body was eating him up. He never knew when they were going to come for him and split him open. He was terrified of ending up in the ground, buried nine feet under dirt all alone.

But even more, he was terrified that the woman would come back. She had been there, whispering in his ear just like she had done on the day of the accident, when she had suddenly been whispering in his ear in the darkness of the theater lobby. Mads had never been so scared in his life.

And now she was here; she knew he was in this bed, but worst of all...she knew he could hear her. She had seen the pinky move, she had to have seen it and then concluded that he could hear her. She knew and yet she didn't tell.

It was beyond cruel.

The nurses laughed and Mads heard their footsteps disappear. Soon followed the well-known sound of the door to his room being closed. He was alone once again in the darkness with nothing but his thoughts for company.

Mads tried to fill his mind with thoughts of happiness to avoid the panic. Most of the times he would go back to the day he met Signe, the happiest day of his life.

He knew her already when he spotted her sitting at the end of a dock at Karrebaeksminde Marina with her feet dangling over the edge and a beer in one hand, a cigarette in the other. Mads had just gotten back from a trip with a friend on his mother's yacht and had just set foot on the dock when he spotted her sitting there. He had heard stories about her. She was the girl whose father had been imprisoned for touching little girls improperly in his classroom and everybody knew he had done bad things to his daughter as well. He knew she had been thrown out of every school she ever attended and now she had to work full-time at the hospital kiosk selling newspapers and get-well-cards. She was scum, the lowest of the lowest in the small society. She was trouble and the one everyone was told by their parents to stay away from.

And that was exactly what attracted him to her. She was different. Nothing like the girls his mother wanted him to be with. She was interesting and exciting. At that second, standing on the dock looking at her sitting there drinking her beer and smoking a cigarette, he felt so drawn to her.

She must have felt him staring at her because she turned her head and looked him in the eyes with that tough look that he later came to love and fear so much.

"What are you staring at, rich boy?" she asked.

Mads had blushed, but couldn't stop looking at her. Her face was so fair and delicate, the lips like small red cherries and her eyes were sparkling with anger and hatred for the world. It was enthralling.

"You," he simply answered.

She smoked her cigarette while looking at him and scrutinizing him. She frightened and captivated him at the same time. It was overpowering.

"Well, stop," she said, blowing out smoke through her nose. "It's freaking me out. If you want something, just say it, rich boy."

"Can I have a cigarette?" he asked with a shivering voice.

She looked up at him again, looking at him like she was about to burst into laughter. He was afraid she might be able to tell from his face that he had never smoked a cigarette in his life.

"Sure," she said. "Here, catch." She threw the package of cigarettes at him and he caught it mid-air. She looked impressed. He took one out and squatted next to her so she could light it with her lighter. He drew in a deep breath and swallowed a cough. He could feel how his face was turning red.

"It's okay to cough," she said with a grin.

Mads had coughed so badly it sounded like he would hack up a lung.

"First time, huh?" she asked.

He chuckled and smoked again. "Yeah. Pretty pathetic, huh?"

"I can think of worse things," she said. "Say, do you like to have some fun?"

His face lit up in a grin. "What did you have in mind?"

Mads was pulled out of his daydream as the door once again was opened to his room at the hospital. He listened carefully to the steps approaching, thinking he would be able to tell if it was the woman again. But it wasn't. And it wasn't one person who entered...it sounded like two. They were talking to each other as they approached the bed. Mads felt they were really close now and he recognized one of the voices. The female one. She had been there before.

"I'll check the left leg if you take the right," she said. "It might be just a small stab-wound."

I'm here. I'm awake. Please see me. Please see me moving my finger!

Mads was screaming helplessly inside of his own mind while desperately trying to move his pinky.

Please see it. Please see my finger! I'm alive. I'm not dead!

"Do you see anything?" the female voice asked.

"There are a lot of scratches and bruises, but they look like they're from the accident," a male voice answered.

I'm moving my finger. I'm moving it now. Can't you see it?

"Yeah, I know. What we're looking for should be deeper if he was stabbed with something." The woman sighed deeply. "Maybe we should ask one of the doctors. Maybe they noticed one of the wounds looked different than what you normally get from being hit by a car?"

"Wait a minute," the male voice said.

Mads felt how his gown was lifted higher up and someone touched his leg. Oh how badly he wanted them to realize he felt everything and heard it all.

"What?" the female voice asked.

Mads heard her move to the other side of his bed.

"This here looks strange. Here on his thigh."

"Yeah. It looks like when a nurse tries to find a vein in your arm but misses and you get a big bruise. It looks like an ordinary bruise, but you can see where the needle tried to penetrate the skin. Maybe a really bad nurse had trouble here at the hospital?"

"Wouldn't they usually use an arm?"

"Maybe they couldn't find any more veins? I don't know; I'm not a nurse," the woman said.

"Neither was this person," the man said. "Just look at it. It looks terrible. There is a wound where the needle went through."

"Yeah. It looks like it was bleeding when it was done," the woman said. "Look at the dried-up blood."

"Could that be it?" the male said. "Could that be what they were talking about? You know that Mads was limping when he stormed outside."

"I don't know. Stephen Pars said it was just a few drops of blood, so I guess it could have been."

Mads was laughing with delight inside his head. Finally, someone was making progress. Finally, someone was figuring out what had happened to him.

Yes! Yes! Yes! He yelled with all his strength. *Yes she tried to inject something into my thigh. Yes, she did it. Please find her, before I die. Please find her!*

"Let's go talk to the doctor," the female voice said.

Mads heard steps, then one of them stopped. "What was that?" the female voice said.

"What was what?" the man asked.

Had they heard him? Had they heard him scream?

"I turned to look at him and I could have sworn that...I...It looked exactly like he was moving the tip of his pinky."

She saw that? She saw it? Yes, yes yes. I'm moving my pinky. Yes, she saw it. Yes, I'm alive, hello? I'm in here? I'm trapped in here! Call the doctor and let them know.

"I didn't see anything," the man said. "Maybe it was a spasm or something."

"Yeah you're probably right. I just can't escape the feeling that..."

"That what?" the man asked.

"I don't know what it is...I just feel like...like he can hear us or something."

I can hear you. I hear everything.

The man chuckled. "That's silly."

"I know. Let's go find the doctor and ask him about the bruise on his thigh."

No. No. Don't go. Don't leave me in this darkness. You saw it. You saw me move my finger. You know I'm alive! Don't leave me!

But the room had already gone as silent as the grave Mads feared so desperately that he'd end up in.

No! Come back!

29

APRIL 2014

Morten and I found Doctor Faaborg in the hallway and he showed us into his office. I had spoken to him on several occasions while worrying about Mads Schou dying and making my daughter a murderer. He was a very nice man in his mid-fifties.

"Now Emma, what can I do for you?" he asked. "Have they located your daughter yet?"

"Not yet, doctor. We're working on it."

"I'm sorry there wasn't more I could do to save Mads Schou...for all who have been involved in this tragedy."

"I'm sure you did all you could," I said, thinking about what I had seen in that room. I couldn't escape the thought that Mads had moved the tip of his pinky. What did it mean? Could he be alive? Could he be trying to signal us?

Come on, Emma. Get real. That kind of stuff only happens in movies. You're being silly.

"So how can I help you today?" the doctor asked, as he looked at his watch. I knew he was a busy man and I had to hurry up.

"We were just wondering about a bruise on Mads Schou's thigh," I said.

"Yes, what about it?" the doctor asked.

"It looks like he had some sort of injection or something?"

The doctor frowned. "In the thigh? I don't think so. I see no reason why a nurse would do that in his thigh."

"He's not diabetic or something, is he?" I asked, thinking briefly about Mrs. Alonzo, the woman onboard the cruise ship who fainted because she forgot to eat in worry about her son.

"No. He is not." The doctor tapped on his keyboard quickly, then looked back at us. "I have the report here and it does say he has a bruise on the right thigh, but according to this, it was caused by the accident. I have no reason to believe that it's not."

"Could you take a look at it?" I asked. "I know you're busy and everything, but it would be a big help to us if you did this."

Doctor Faaborg looked at me and smiled. I knew he liked me. He loved my books and had read all of them, he had told me on several occasions.

"I can send you a signed copy of my book?" I said.

"Now, Emma Frost," he said chuckling. "That's bribing. But okay. I'll do this for you and you could choose to give me the book afterwards as a present."

"Sounds perfect."

We got up from his office chairs and followed doctor Faaborg back to Mads' room. I hated walking through that door. It constantly reminded me that somewhere out there Maya was feeling awful and scared to death about what had happened. I loathed myself for ever having told her to hang up the phone, but I knew there was nothing else I could have done. I just couldn't escape the thought that maybe if I had stayed with her, then she would never have disappeared. But it was so easy to blame yourself in hindsight.

"Let me show you where it is," I said, as we walked to Mads' lifeless body. I hated the sound of all the monitors and pumps keeping him alive. There was just something about this whole thing that felt really bad to me. Maybe it was just being face to face with death like this, face to face with the fact that life was so short, so fragile.

I pulled the covers off of him again and pulled his gown up to show the bruise. The doctor leaned over and examined it closely.

"I do believe you're right," he grunted. "It looks like an injection bruise instead of a bruise cause by a blow. But it is very hard to tell. They're very similar. There appears to be an injection hole, though, which indicates it might have been made by an injection, yes."

"Do you know if any of your nurses could have done this?" I asked.

Doctor Faaborg shook his head and looked at me with a compassionate smile. "I really couldn't tell. We have so many nurses coming in and out of here all day."

I exhaled, disappointed. I had hoped for a more direct answer. What we got was nothing certain, but a maybe that brought us nowhere.

"Okay. Well thank you for your time," I said.

Morten was about to shake the doctor's hand, when he suddenly made a strange shriek. "Did you see that?"

"See what?" I asked.

"It looked like his finger moved!" Morten looked at me like he had seen a ghost.

The doctor put his glasses on and went to the other side of Mads' body to look more closely.

"Right there," Morten said and pointed. "The pinky. It was only the tip, but I am positive he moved it."

The doctor stared at the pinky for a long time, but nothing happened. My heart was beating faster now.

"I saw it too," I said, full of hope. Could he really have moved it on purpose? Was he trying to tell us something? Could he be alive after all? "When we were in here earlier."

"Hm," the doctor said and examined Mads' hand and arm. He let it fall flat back on the bed. "Still seems lifeless." He took off his glasses and looked at me. "It's probably just reflex muscle jerks or twitches. It's not unusual."

"But what if it's not?" I asked. "What if he's alive?"

Doctor Faaborg chuckled. "No. He's not alive. Of that I'm certain. He's completely brain-dead, but I will run a few more tests to be certain."

30

APRIL 2012

They didn't dare to stay in Alanya. Not so much because they were afraid of the police coming after them for killing those men in the street. No, they were scared of the family members and friends of those they had killed...other gang members coming after them to avenge their deaths. Someone could have seen what happened. There were eyes on every corner of streets like those.

So as soon as Signe felt good enough, they booked a plane out of there. They decided to go to Monaco. The small kingdom by the Mediterranean Sea occupied by casinos and multi-million-dollar-yachts. It was Mads' idea. He had been there once before with his friends when they just turned eighteen and were allowed inside the casinos. They booked a suite at Hotel Hermitage Monte-Carlo and soon threw themselves onto the king-sized bed. Mads was smiling happily. These were his kind of people; he felt at home while Signe felt estranged. Like she didn't belong. She was certain the snobbish man behind the counter downstairs had seen it on her when they checked in. He looked at her bruises like she was some hooker Mads had bought for the night.

"Have you seen this view?" Signe asked and pulled away the heavy curtain. She had never been in a place quite like this. The building itself looked like something a Russian Czar could have built. "Is that the ocean?"

Mads chuckled and came up behind her. He hugged her and held her tight. She froze. Physical affection had always been hard for her. She never knew what he wanted out of it. She wondered if he was going to have sex with her now and prepared herself mentally for it. But he didn't try anything. He didn't pull her pants down and bend her over the bed and force himself on her like she expected. He never did anything like that and it made Signe nervous. She never knew how to react. Was it because he didn't desire her enough? Wasn't she desirable? It wasn't that they didn't have sex. It was just so different than what she was used to. She didn't like it. It made her insecure. And since she'd been sick from the beating, Mads hadn't tried to get close to her, not even once in almost a week. It was breaking her heart. She wasn't used to men being careful with her. Her dad never was. Even if he had badly bruised her, he would still force himself on her. It was her own fault, he had told her back then...for making herself so desirable. He constantly wanted her and that had made her feel like she was loved. He told her himself that it was because he loved her so much that he wanted to be close to her.

Didn't Mads love her anymore?

Signe turned and kissed him passionately. "Take me," she whispered. "Fuck me right here."

"Not now," Mads said and pulled away. "You're still healing, remember? I don't want to hurt you."

Signe frowned. "You don't want to hurt me? Why not? Don't you love me?"

"What on earth do you mean?" Mads asked.

"You don't want to be with me."

He grabbed her shoulders and looked into her eyes. "Signe, I love you. That's why I want to take care of you and make sure you're not hurt. Don't you understand?"

She shook her head. "No. I want you to fuck me." She grabbed his belt and started to undo it. It had always worked on her father if he was angry or upset. She pulled Mads' pants down and took it out. It was just hanging there. Signe gasped. It wasn't even erect. It was true then. He didn't desire her anymore. He didn't love her.

"Signe, not now," Mads said and pulled his pants back up.

She shook her head in desperation. A knot of tears grew in her throat. She tried to swallow it, but could hardly speak.

"I...I...." She turned her back on him then stormed out on the balcony where she burst into tears.

Mads came out after her. He handed her a cigarette. "Here," he said with a smile. She looked up at him.

"Care for a smoke?"

She sniffled and took one. She felt confused as she drew in the smoke. Mads was so nice to her. Why was he being so nice? What did it mean?

"I was thinking we could hit a couple of casinos tonight," he said, blowing smoke out into the fresh salty air. "Have a little fun again, huh? It's been a while since I've seen you smile. I know you like to have fun. Let's spend an insane amount of money and make my mother really angry once she finds out, huh?"

Signe smoked and felt better. She liked the idea. It did always make her feel better to spend money. She didn't care that they would probably end up using all the money they had been given to buy the house. She never felt like it was hers anyway.

"Okay," she said. "Let's rock and roll."

"Now there's the smile I've missed so much."

31

APRIL 2014

"We've been trying to track down Signe Schou while you guys were gone," Rebekka said, as we came back to the office. "But we haven't found out much so far. Only that she never showed up at the theater. I talked to her mother on the phone, but she told me she hasn't seen Signe in two years. Not since they were married and went on their honeymoon. I don't know if she was telling the truth, though. She didn't seem like the most dependable type, if you know what I mean. She could be lying... maybe to protect her daughter."

I rubbed my forehead and sat down on a chair. Morten poured me some coffee.

"Thanks," I whispered and received a gentle smile in return.

Morten sat down as well. He could sense my tension. I couldn't bear the thought that another day was almost gone and I still hadn't come much closer to finding Maya. I kept looking at my phone, expecting her to call or text at any moment. If she was alive and hiding, she would contact me eventually, wouldn't she? I was afraid she was too scared. Maybe she thought I would be angry with her or something. I couldn't stand not knowing.

"So, what did you get out of your visit to the hospital?" Rebekka asked.

I exhaled sharply. "Not much really. It looks like he had some sort of injection in his thigh, one that left a bad bruise, but the doctor couldn't tell if it had happened at the hospital or at another time. It was really ugly though and didn't look very professional. It had been bleeding too. There was a lot of dried up blood surrounding it. But I don't know what it means or if it is really important."

"It could explain his limp," Sune said without looking up from his computer screen. "If the person who attacked him injected something and caused the bruise."

"That's what I thought too," Morten said.

"Yeah, well it doesn't explain where Maya is," I said with another deep sigh. I was starting to lose hope and that wasn't good. I sipped my coffee, trying hard not to imagine Maya in trouble somewhere. I had closed my eyes for a second when my phone suddenly rang. I grabbed it. It was my dad's cell. He called every day at this hour when Victor came home from school. It was important for Victor that it was at the exact same time every day.

"Hi sweetie," he said. "How are things? Getting any better?"

"I can't say they are. How's everything at home? How's Victor?"

"He's good. A little trouble at school, but we'll talk about it when you get back. Focus on what's important now. He wants to say hi to you."

"Put him on."

"Hi mom," he said, sounding all of a sudden so grown up. He was about to turn nine soon, so I guess he was growing up as well. I just had a harder time letting go of him than Maya, since he had always taken so much of my attention. I suddenly wished that he would never get older, that he would always stay my sweet innocent Victor.

"Hi, sweetheart. How was your day?"

"You asked me this yesterday," he answered.

"Yes, but today is a new day. How was this day?"

"I really don't like answering the same question again. Can't you come up with a new one?"

"Okay," I said. I couldn't help smiling. Victor never changed and I was suddenly so thrilled he didn't. "So how about you tell me how it is to be with Grandpa and Grandma?"

"It's good, I guess. They're nice."

"Aren't you going to ask me how I'm doing?"

"Why?"

"Because that's the polite thing to do. It shows you're interested in others."

"But I'm not," he said, like it was the most natural thing in the world.

"Okay, buddy. I'm glad to hear you're doing well," I said.

"Thank you."

"That was very polite."

"I know. Can I go now?"

"Okay, buddy. Put your granddad back on."

"So, no news about Maya?" my dad asked as soon as he was back.

"Not yet. It's getting really hard."

"I know. But you have to hang in there. You can't give up. It'll all be fine. I know it will...Wait a second, Victor looks odd." My dad's voice became weaker. I could hear him talking to Victor in the background. Then my dad returned. "Victor is saying something. I don't quite grasp it, but he says it's for you."

"What is it?"

"He said to tell you he likes rats? That's what he said. *Tell her I like pet rats.*"

I chuckled. "Tell him we'll discuss it when I get back."

32

APRIL 2014

"So what else did you find out about Signe Schou?" Morten asked, when I had hung up and put the phone down.

"Anything we can use?"

Rebekka looked through her notes. "We know she had a terrible childhood and that Mads' mother tried to pay her off, but that's pretty much it. She went to the local high school for just a few months, then was thrown out and had to work to earn money until she met Mads and married him."

"They were married in 2012, right?" I asked.

"Yes," Rebekka said.

"So what has she been doing since?"

Rebekka threw her arms out. "Beats me. Everyone we have spoken to tells us she married Mads and then they never saw her again. They went on a honeymoon to Egypt for a month or so. Neither the mother nor her few friends have seen her since."

"But she was active on Facebook recently," I said.

"That's right," Rebekka said and sipped her coffee. "Maybe she's just been enjoying life and spending her husband's money."

"What about Mads? What has he been doing?" I asked.

"He's been working in his dad's company since mid-May 2012,

according to the company's profile. He's supposed to take over when his dad retires. Lundbit. It's a pharmaceutical company. Lots of money involved."

"Wasn't there a scandal once?" Sune asked.

"Yes," Rebekka replied. "They were accused some years ago of trying to bribe doctors to select their medicine above other brands. It's illegal in this country, you know. Nevertheless they've been accused of owning some doctors in the Danish hospitals. But those are just rumors. They've never been convicted of anything."

I looked at my phone again, hoping and praying for Maya to call me and for this nightmare to be finally over. Things were getting too complicated and I felt like we were getting further and further away from my daughter. I was scared that we were using our energy on the wrong things here. We had to focus on what happened after they all ran out of the theater. Who was that woman who followed Mads and pushed him in front of the car?

"I know what you're thinking," Rebekka suddenly said. "And believe me I know how it feels. You're worried that we're focusing on the wrong things, right? Well, I think we're on to something. I think that in order to find this woman who pushed Mads into the street, we need to figure out why she attacked Mads. It might have something to do with his wife, who also seems to have vanished. So I don't believe we're wasting our time, even if it seems so, okay? Trust me on this."

I finished my coffee. "You're right," I said with a thick voice. I fought hard to pull myself up and concentrate on the task ahead. "We need to work with what we've got."

"Exactly." Rebekka put a hand on my shoulder. "We're going to find her. I'll do everything I can. And I'm sure the police will do more now that Sascha DuBois has told them about the woman. They'll find her."

"What do we do until then?" Sune asked.

"If she was at the party," I said and looked at my friends. "If the woman was at the party, then she must be on the list, right? She must be on the Facebook-list for the event. How many were there who said they would attend? Twenty?"

Sune tapped on his keyboard. "Twenty-three," he said.

"How many were women?"

Sune looked again. "Looks like about half of them. Maybe a little less."

"So you believe she is one of them?" Rebekka asked.

"How else could she have known about the party?" I asked. "How could she have known Mads was attending this thing?"

"I'll print out the profile on each of the participants who are women," Sune said and let his fingers dance across the keyboard. "Then we'll take a look at them one after another and see if anything jumps out at us as strange or as a possible profile."

33

APRIL 2012

Signe forgot everything about feeling sad once they hit the Casino de Monte Carlo. It started out so well for them. One win after another. Everything turned in their favor. The balls in the wheels, the cards, even the slot machines seemed to welcome them to the small kingdom with favor and open arms.

After just a few hours, they had tripled the amount they started with. Mads and Signe enjoyed themselves immensely, shoveling money in and drinking the free drinks served to them.

"It must be you," Mads said with a grin as they went to roll the dice. "You're my lucky charm. I've never won anything before at a casino. A little here and a little there, but nothing as major as this. You and me together, baby. It's just a lucky combination."

Signe liked seeing him happy like this and enjoyed the excitement of gambling these big amounts, big numbers, big enough to make anyone's hands shake as they rolled the dice.

"You do it," Mads said and handed them to her. "Roll me an eight."

In that moment, his eyes sparkled with love for her. She took the dice and threw them.

"Eight!" the croupier yelled.

Signe jumped and clapped. Mads grabbed her and kissed her. "You're amazing. You know that? You're so amazing."

Signe couldn't stop laughing as more money was rolled to their side of the table. "Eight again," Mads said. "Do it again and we can travel to the Caribbean and spend the rest of our lives there."

He was drunk now. Signe could see it in his eyes. They were drowsy, but happy and sparkling with excitement.

"Just one more time," he whispered. "Do it for me. Come on, baby."

Signe lifted her arm and threw the dice. They jumped across the green table and took forever to lie still. The croupier looked at them, then up at Signe and Mads.

"It's an eight!" he yelled.

Everyone around the table burst into a loud cheer. Mads turned to Signe, then picked her up and swung her in his arms. "We're rich, Signe. We're truly rich! This time, it's no longer my parent's money. It's our own, Signe. This is ours!"

Signe laughed and kissed him, thinking this was the happiest moment of her life. Finally, they could escape from her mother in-law's sharp claws. Finally, they could take care of themselves and never go back to that boring country. Finally, she would get the life she deserved, and after everything that had happened to her, after everything she had been through, it was only fair.

Mads put her down and kissed her again. He grabbed two drinks from a waitress and gave one to Signe.

"To us," he said. "YNWA."

They clinked their glasses and drank. "What was that you said?" Signe asked. She watched as Mads emptied the entire glass and grabbed another one as another waitress walked by. "What's that?"

"Those letters you said. What do they mean?"

"YNWA?"

She nodded and sipped her drink. She was getting very drunk now. Whether it was the overwhelming joy, the ambiance, or the alcohol, she didn't know, but it felt like a dream.

"It stands for *You'll Never Walk Alone*. It's Liverpool's fan-song. I think it fits us so well. You and me baby. We'll always be together. You'll never be alone again."

Signe looked at her husband and had no idea what to say. She now realized they really were made for one another. He wasn't just some rich guy that she had gotten her claws into like her mother had said. He wasn't just her way out of the miserable slum. They were actually compatible. Even if he had the facade of the nice pretty boy, Mads was just as crazy and unpredictable as she was.

She loved that about him. She loved everything about him in this second. Right up until that petrifying moment later when he said the few words destined to change everything:

"Now let's try roulette."

34

APRIL 2014

I was on the phone most of the afternoon calling all the women on the list that agreed to talk to me. None of them really wanted to talk much about what had happened at the party. They all seemed to believe it had only been a cruel joke, a prank that someone had played on them, and to be frank, they were pissed off at whoever had arranged the party. I kept asking them if they knew who it was, but none of them did. None of them knew where Signe Schou was either. They all seemed to know who she was, but no one had seen Signe since her wedding.

I hung up feeling more lost than ever. I looked at Rebekka who had also just hung up and was now approaching me with a serious look in her eyes. It frightened me a little.

"What's wrong?" I asked.

"I just got off the phone with Karrebaeksminde Police. I was trying to get an update on the case of the hit and run hoping to hear that they were now investigating it as an attempted murder case and that they were now looking for the woman who pushed Mads Schou in front of the car."

"But they weren't?" I asked.

Rebekka shook her head. "Not even close. They haven't heard anything about it. Nothing about any woman or anyone being pushed."

My hands started shaking in anger. "She didn't talk to them? Sascha hasn't told them anything?"

"Apparently not. Maybe you should get ahold of her once again," Rebekka said.

"She promised me she would do it right away. I don't understand," I said, puzzled. Sascha had seemed so convincing. I had no doubt in my mind that she was going to do it. Why hadn't she been down there to talk to them yet? Had she lied to me? Just to get me off her back? Had she backed out? Had fear overcome her?

"Let me get to the bottom of this," I said, as I grabbed my purse and stormed towards the door. Morten got up and followed me.

"I'll go with you," he said.

I heard concern in his voice. It was sweet. He was worried.

"Thanks," I said.

We drove to Sascha's apartment in silence. I felt anger and worry at the same time. I simply couldn't understand why she hadn't done as promised. I parked the car close to her building and we both got out. I felt more and more anxious as I approached the building. Something wasn't right here. Something was off.

I opened the door and we went up the stairs, taking two steps at a time. When we reached her platform, I froze. The door to her apartment was ajar.

Cautiously, I walked closer and pushed the door open.

"Hello? Sascha?"

No answer.

I walked inside and looked around. The apartment looked just like it had when we left it. There was no sign of Sascha DuBois. I rubbed my forehead and let out a frustrated sound.

"You think she bailed on us?" Morten asked. "You think she's run away?"

I walked into the bedroom and found her clothes in the closet hanging neatly on hangers. "Wouldn't she have taken her clothes with her?"

He shrugged. "Not if you're really afraid and want to hurry."

I walked back into the kitchen. A tray of cups was on the counter. I walked closer and looked into them. "They're ours," I said. "I put a small gum wrapper into mine before we left. It's still there. She never got to clean them."

"So you think she left right after we were here?"

I shook my head. "I have a strange feeling about this..."

"What do you mean?"

"Something is definitely off." I walked to the small table next to the door to the hallway. On the small table, Sascha kept her keys and...I picked something up and showed it to Morten. "I don't believe she would run off without her wallet, do you?" I opened it and looked inside. "There's credit cards and cash in here. I don't think she would have left all this if she had run off, do you?"

Morten shook his head. "Probably not. So what do you think happened?"

I looked around, then walked back into the hallway. I put my finger on the inside of the door. There was a bump. I touched it with my finger. "Someone was in here," I said and looked at my finger. Then I showed it to Morten.

"Is that blood?" he asked.

"I'm afraid so. The door was slammed into her face. Look there's blood on the floor over here as well. Small droplets that have sunk into the wood. She must have fallen. My guess is that someone took her out of here right after we were here."

Morten looked terrified. "Who? Who would have done this?"

"My guess is that it's a woman. The same woman that pushed Mads Schou out in front of the car."

35

APRIL 2014

"Did you find her and talk to her?" Rebekka asked as we stormed back inside the office.

"Not exactly," Morten answered.

I threw myself into a chair and stared for a long time at the chocolate cake in the middle of the table. Sara was eating a piece of it with great pleasure.

"You want some?" she asked with a big smile.

"Yes, please," I said, thinking if Morten made as much as one little remark, I was going to kill him. This piece of cake was what I needed right now. I was frustrated and angry and wanted to scream at the top of my lungs, scream at the world at how unfair I thought everything was. But I simply wasn't the type. It wasn't my thing. Instead, I drowned my anger with a nice giant piece of rich chocolate cake. I knew it was bad, but I couldn't help it. I wasn't able to, all of a sudden, get some self-control in a situation like this. Sara handed me a fork and I started eating.

"What happened?" Rebekka asked and came closer. Sune grabbed a piece of cake as well. Rebekka and Morten soon followed.

"She's gone," Morten said before he shoveled in his first bite.

I nodded and swallowed. "Sascha DuBois never made it to the police station. I think she was right to be afraid. She told me she hadn't gone to the police because she was afraid of the woman she had seen, afraid she would come after her next. I fear that she was right."

"So, she didn't just run off?" Sune asked.

I sipped my coffee, then shook my head. "No. She left everything in the apartment. Wallet, credit cards, cash, clothes everything."

"She hadn't even cleaned the cups we had used when we visited her. We think she might have been attacked soon afterwards."

Rebekka looked terrified. "That's awful."

"I know," I said.

"At least we now know for sure that we're on to something here," Sune said. "Something even the police have no clue about."

"We should call Officer Hansen," Morten said. "We have to tell him everything we know."

"But we have no proof, and now our only witness to the murder attempt is missing as well. What do you want us to tell them?" I asked. "They already think I'm just a lunatic mother who refuses to believe my daughter could do anything wrong."

Morten nodded pensively while eating. "You have a point. Maybe if I talk to them alone?"

"That sounds like a great idea," Rebekka said. "Then we'll focus on finding this mysterious woman on our own."

"Any news?" I asked.

Rebekka shook her head. "Not really. We've been through every woman on the list from Facebook. We've spoken to all of them."

"Except one," I said.

"Who's that?"

"Signe Schou. I'm guessing you haven't gotten an answer from her, right?" I said.

"You got that right. She hasn't been on Facebook since the day of the party and her mother hasn't seen her for a very long time."

"What about Mads' mother?" Sune suddenly asked. "Pennie Schou?"

"What about her?" I asked puzzled.

"Could she have done any of this?" Sune continued.

"I don't understand," Rebekka said.

Sune leaned over the table. He looked very mysterious. I sensed he enjoyed this kind of work.

"I'm just saying that we know she tried to pay off Signe Schou to not marry her son. She was against the marriage all along. Could she have made Signe Schou disappear somehow?"

"You mean, she thought her son was such a disgrace that she got rid of the daughter in law?" Rebekka asked. "Then she went to the son and, when he got angry and didn't want to be a part of it or to do as he was told, she ran after him and pushed him out in front of a car in anger?"

"Why at a party?" I asked.

"Maybe she knew he would be there," Sune said. "Maybe he refused to have anything to do with her or even speak to her anymore and she knew she had to sneak up on him to be able to get him to talk to her. Maybe she was even the one who turned off the lights?"

"But the guy standing close to him said they were fighting and then Mads was hurt," Morten said. "You think she just came there to kill him?"

Rebekka and Sune both shrugged. "We've seen stranger things," she said.

I felt intrigued by this theory. I left the rest of my cake and got up from my chair.

"Where are you going now?" Morten asked.

"To have a chat with this Pennie Schou."

36

APRIL 2012

Signe spent all night trying to stop him, but he wouldn't listen. It was like he was all of a sudden possessed with something evil making him want to continue, no matter how much he lost. And he did lose. He lost a lot. Four hours passed and not a single win. Signe was about to cry when she realized that, not only had he lost everything they'd won, he had lost a lot more than that and soon they were escorted out of the casino by the security guards and left in the street.

They walked back to the hotel and the next morning they woke up to a very disturbing message from Mads' mother telling them that she was on to them and that she had cut them off. She had closed all of their credit cards and told the bank not to give them any more money, should they contact them.

They were broke.

"What are we going to do?" Signe asked with a shivering voice after they had both read the e-mail.

Mads was still in so much shock from the huge loss that he had hardly said anything all morning. Signe slapped him on his shoulder.

"Talk to me, Mads. You have to do something. We don't have any credit cards and no cash. How are we going to pay for this room? How are we going to eat today? How are we going to get money? We lost everything from our account that was supposed to go to the house, your mom cut us off and we even owe money to the casino from last night. They gave us three days to get the money. We can't come up with that amount of money in three days, Mads. Even if we sell everything we have. Even if we sell my ring, it won't be enough. They're going to kill us. What are we going to do? Answer me, goddammit!"

Mads hid his face in his hands. "I...I...I don't know. I've never been in a situation like this. I've never been without money before."

"Well I have," Signe said. "But I never thought I'd be in this situation again. I thought it was over. I thought I never had to worry about money again for the rest of my life."

Mads looked up and into her eyes. His look terrified her.

"Is that why you married me? Was my mother right about you?" he asked.

Signe hesitated. She didn't know what to say. She was completely unprepared for the question and had no answer ready. "No...no...," she said, but he interrupted her.

"I think I'm beginning to understand." Mads got up. He still had that look in his eyes. The look of distrust. "She was right, wasn't she? You married me to get away from the slum. You just said it. You married me to get someone to take care of you for the rest of your life so you didn't have to worry about money anymore. I've been fooling myself thinking you actually loved me, haven't I? My mother warned me about girls like you all of my life, and still I fell right into your little trap. Was it even an accident that we met that day on the dock? Were you waiting for me? Had your mother told you to sit there so I would see you?"

Signe shook her head. "No Mads. It was nothing like that."

"I don't believe you. What about the fake pregnancy, huh? Did your mother come up with that as well?"

Signe hesitated. He was right. Her mother had come up with that. It was her idea for her to marry Mads and be secure forever. But Signe couldn't tell him that. He wouldn't understand. He wouldn't understand that she had originally wanted him for the money, but now she had grown to love him. She didn't know much about love or how to do it, but she did know she couldn't bear to lose him. She did know she would be lost without him. She would be devastated.

"Mads. You know me. I love you. I wanted to marry you because I loved you. You and me, baby. We belong together, remember? YNWA."

Mads seemed calmer. Signe leaned over him and looked deeply into his eyes. Then she kissed him passionately to make him forget everything. He grabbed her and carried her back to the bed where he pulled off her clothes and tied her down using his shirt. Then he rode her wildly and without any consideration of her needs like he usually did. He was rough with her and slapped her face, then threw himself at her and didn't stop, even when she told him it hurt.

Signe gasped and let him have his way with her like she had done with her father so many times. She closed her eyes and felt calm as he punched her in the face. Finally, he had become the beast she wanted him to be. Finally, the pretty boy was gone. Finally, he was showing her how much he loved her. This was a language she understood. This was what she believed to be real love.

"YNWA," she whispered as he came inside of her and his body writhed in spasms.

"YNWA," he whispered back once he caught his breath.

And that was when she had the idea. She opened her eyes and stared into his. "I know what to do," she said. "I know exactly what we can do."

37

APRIL 2014

The numerologist was walking down the hallway looking satisfied at the numbers on the row of doors.

"Sixty-five," she mumbled to herself. "Six plus five is eleven. Eleven is a Master number."

The numerologist giggled and rubbed her hands. She loved eleven more than anything. Whenever she came across this specific Master number she always felt a thrill of excitement. She stopped in front of the door with the number sixty-five, then reached her hand out and gently touched the number on the door. Then she smiled.

"So powerful," she mumbled. "If only people understood how powerful you are."

When she was in prison, she had also been in room sixty-five. Back then she knew nothing about how powerful numbers were, but today she understood. Today she knew that there was a reason why she had been in that room. Even with all that happened to her while she was there, she now knew that it was only because she didn't understand the power of the numbers. She didn't realize that she wasn't a victim back then. She thought she had no power, no control. But if only she had been able to draw the energy from the numbers, she would never have been the victim, she would have been the one in control of it all.

But that was many years ago now. And today, she knew so much more and she wanted others to know it as well. She wanted others just like her to stop being victims and start being powerful.

"You have to choose," she always told them. "Either you're pitiful or you're powerful. You can't be both."

The numerologist had been pitiful. Back in her teenage years when she was put in prison. She had seen herself as a victim. She hadn't wanted to change her ways, she hadn't understood what the universe was trying to tell her.

Now she was passing it on to others. The message through the numbers. They had been speaking to her all through her life, telling her what to do and yet she never listened because she never knew. She never saw them. She had no idea. Not until many years later when she came across a book about numerology that opened her eyes to the power available to her in this universe.

The numerologist opened the door and walked inside the room. The girl sitting in the chair didn't even look up as she entered. The numerologist smiled and walked inside. She closed the door and locked it behind her.

"Hello, Lot. How are you? I hear you're having trouble sleeping?"

"I want to leave this place," the girl said. "I don't belong here."

The numerologist grabbed a chair and sat down. "Now, why do you say that?"

"I don't know. I just think I have somewhere to be. I think I need to do something...that someone is waiting for me. I...I...have this feeling that...." Lot hid her face between her hands.

"Lot, you..."

"See, that's it again," she interrupted.

The numerologist snorted. She didn't like to be interrupted. It was so rude. But again, she had to think about this girls' background. It was very similar to her own. That was why she understood her better than the others.

"What is?"

"I can't put my finger on it, but there is something..." The girl turned her head and looked at the numerologist. "There is something wrong about that name."

"What name is that?"

"Lot. You keep calling me that, but I don't feel like...It's like it's not my real name or something."

The numerologist scoffed. "Well, that's just your illness talking. Remember why you're here. You are suffering and I'm trying to help you."

"I know...I know. It's just...I can't shake the feeling that there was something I was supposed to do. Somewhere I was supposed to be."

"Well, that's just nonsense," the numerologist scoffed. "That is simply your mind playing tricks on you. You're exactly where you need to be. You got yourself in trouble and I helped you out. You're here to straighten your life out. That's all you need to know."

"But...but I don't remember anything? I don't remember how I was in trouble. What did I do that was so bad?"

"You don't need to remember the details. It's not time now to focus on the past. We're looking towards the future now, looking forward towards your new life. Now let's look at the number eleven..."

"And what's with the rat in my room? That cage over there. It keeps me awake all night. It makes too much noise."

"She. Not it. It's a she. I believe rats are calming for the soul. She's in here because it's good for you to have some company. You can take her out every now and then if you want to. She's your companion now. Now, back to the number. Eleven. It keeps popping up around you. It's the number of your room, it's the number of your name and this morning I realized it is also your number of the day. I think it means something special. I think you're going to make big progress today. Now, let's begin with what we know about the Master number eleven. The numerology meanings for number eleven must be analyzed from its structure. It is made up of two ones. As number one represents Sun, you are ruled twice by the sun. As such, you are unselfish, dutiful, and altruistic, in your nature. Number eleven is hailed as a Master Number. It has special powers to give you remarkable intelligence and wisdom. You plan your activities well and always aim for excellence." The numerologist paused and looked at the girl to make sure she was following her. Then she continued:

"Now to the dark side. Numerology meanings for eleven indicate that, like the moon never reveals its dark side, you too have a secret aspect in your personality, which you never reveal. It makes you nurse secret fears about others around you. You're very afflicted by the numbers nine and eight. If you meet it as either your day number or in someone's life number, then don't make important decisions. If you meet someone with the number nine or eight in their name, stay away from them, they will only cause you your ruin."

The numerologist looked at the girl again. She seemed pensive. That was a good sign. She was processing the information.

"Mads," the girl suddenly said.

The numerologist froze. She stared at the girl. How could this be? How could she remember that name?

"No," she said. "Mads is the number ten. That's not one to..."

The girl shook her head. "No, no. I didn't mean the number. I...I don't know where it came from. I just felt like saying it. Do I know anyone named Mads?"

The numerologist snorted. "Certainly not." She grabbed her book and got up from the chair. "I think we're done for the day."

"But...please stay and tell me. I think there's something I remember, but I don't know what...I want to remember. I want so badly to remember everything. Please stay and help me, please don't leave me," the girl pleaded as the numerologist unlocked the door and opened it. She turned and looked at the girl.

"Please, help me remember? It's terrible to not know anything. I don't even remember my parents. Do I have a boyfriend? Do I have any siblings?" Lot asked with tears in her voice.

"Some things are better left in the past, believe me. You don't want to know," the numerologist said, then closed the door and locked it.

Her heart was beating wildly as she listened to the girl cry behind the door. The numerologist was angry. The girl was so lucky to have finally gotten rid of her past, didn't she understand that? Didn't she know how fortunate she was that she no longer had to be tormented by what had happened to her...that she no longer had to relive those awful moments in her life over and over again? She had been given a second chance, a chance to start all over. How many wouldn't kill to get that?

A man in a white coat approached her outside in the hallway. "How's she doing today?" he asked.

"Not well, I'm afraid. She needs to have her medicine doubled, pronto."

"As you wish, doctor."

38

APRIL 2014

Mads was exhausted. Moving the tip of his pinky had taken up all of his strength. But it had worked, hadn't it? The woman had seen it and so had the man. Now they had told the doctor and he had told them he would run more tests.

At least all hope wasn't lost. Every time Mads heard the door open and feet approach, he waited for them to begin their testing. He was saving his strength for them. Once they started, he would put all he had into moving that pinky like never before. The wait felt unbearable. Why didn't they do anything? Why hadn't they started yet?

The door finally opened and someone approached, but he knew it wasn't a nurse. He recognized the sound of the very expensive high-heeled Manolo Blahniks tapping across the linoleum.

It was his mom. He felt her grab his hand.

"How are you doing this evening, sweetie?" she asked, while touching his face gently.

How do you think I'm doing? I'm terrified.

"The doctor tells me he wants to run some more tests. I'm really excited about that."

Excited? How can you be excited? How can you still love me after all that happened?

Mads heard more footsteps, then another voice close to him. It was his sister. "Don't get your hopes up too high, Mother. They said it was nearly impossible."

"I know, dear. I know. But a mother can hope, can't she?"

Mads felt her stroke his cheek again.

"Look at him," she said. "Lying there all lifeless. He needs a shave again. I don't understand how all this hair can grow when they tell me he's not alive. It doesn't make any sense."

"I'll make sure he gets another shave, Mother. Now you should really go home and get some rest. They won't do any more tests until tomorrow. It's getting late."

"He always was a good boy. Such a good boy."

A good boy? Since when? Don't you remember anything that happened? I failed, mother. I was a disgrace to you all, remember? I shamed our good family name, remember? I deserve all of this.

The door opened and more footsteps approached. A voice said something.

"Mrs. Schou?"

Mads recognized the voice from earlier and his heart jumped with joy. It was the woman again. It was that same woman who had seen him move his pinky when no one else did.

"Yes?" his mother replied. "Oh it's you. Have you come to make more excuses for your daughter's behavior?"

Stop harassing this woman, for crying out loud! Mads yelled inside of his head. He was sick and tired of not being able to tell them all the truth. It was devastating, knowing all he did and not being able to tell anyone.

"No. As a matter of fact I'm here to speak to you. Do you have a second?" the woman asked.

"What on earth for? I'm not the one to blame here," his mother said, sounding appalled.

You're not to blame? Really? If it hadn't been for you, I wouldn't be in this situation.

"No, I didn't say that. I was just wondering about a few things. Maybe if you could clarify them for me, I'd be able to find my daughter and we could have the question of her guilt answered."

Mads heard his mother snort. "Well, not that I have any doubt about her guilt. It's very obvious really, but yes I could answer a few questions if that would help in any way."

"I've been wondering about Mads' wife. Signe Schou. I haven't seen her visit him here in the hospital and I haven't heard about her once since the accident. Do you know where I can reach her?"

Mads felt a tension go through his body at the mention of her name. Signe. How sad he felt all of a sudden.

Why Signe? Why did you do this to us? Why did you have to destroy everything good that we had? Why?

39

APRIL 2014

"We have tried to locate her, isn't that right, Thilde?"

Mads Schou's mother looked tired. Probably from spending every day in the hospital worrying about her son, I thought to myself as I watched her speak.

The sister approached us. "Yes," she said. "I have called everyone possible to try and find her."

Her eyes avoided mine as she spoke. She looked uncomfortable. I couldn't escape the thought that she looked like she was lying.

"So, she's disappeared?" I asked.

The mother smacked her lips. "Well, I probably wouldn't go so far as to say she's disappeared. My guess is that she has taken off. She wasn't much of a wife to my boy, if you understand. They figured that out as soon as they went on that horrible honeymoon. When they came back, they were already sick of each other. The girl isn't well, if you ask me. Too much baggage, if you understand."

"So, she hasn't been here to see Mads at all?"

"No. She hasn't shown her face here and, frankly, we don't care much. She was wrong for my son from the beginning, but how do you tell your only son not to marry the woman he chooses? If you do, you can be certain he will anyway. Do you have any boys, my dear?"

"I do. One," I answered while wondering how they could have grown sick of one another on a honeymoon. It sounded strange. I began thinking that the mother had finally managed to pay off Signe and have her leave. Maybe, if the number was big enough, anyone would cave? Several of the eyewitnesses from the party had told us they heard that Signe and Mads had split up. Was Signe that greedy?

"Were they getting a divorce?" I asked.

The mother looked appalled. "Good Lord, no. We do not accept divorces in our family."

"So they were together after the honeymoon? I don't understand."

The mother's face grew longer and the sister took over.

"It's a family matter," she said, while her mother went to a chair and sat down.

The sister whispered. "But yes, they're still married, technically. Even if they don't live together. When they returned from the honeymoon, they split up. There was no drama to it. Mads didn't love her anymore, he said. Mother made sure the girl never needed for anything. She paid her enough for her to live off the rest of her life. The last I heard, the girl moved back to live with her mother. Mads didn't see her again. He never wanted to. He was really angry with her for some reason. There isn't more to the story than that. Mads wanted a divorce, but mother refused. We don't do divorces in our family. It's a disgrace to the name."

I stared at the woman who was about my age, but seemed so much older. I wasn't surprised that Signe's mother had lied to us about having seen her daughter. I had a feeling she wasn't telling Rebekka the truth.

I looked at my watch and realized it had gotten really late. Morten was waiting outside the hospital room and I knew he badly wanted to go back to the hotel room. But there was something odd about what the sister was telling me, something that didn't add up. If they had no contact. If Mads and Signe didn't see each other anymore, why had they written on each other's Facebook walls? What was it again they had written?

"YNWA," I mumbled.

The mother lifted her head and stared at me. The sister looked at me strangely. "What was that?" she asked.

I shook my head. "Nothing. YNWA is something Liverpool's fans sing. It stands for *You'll Never Walk Alone*. I just remembered it."

I stared at them. They were both extremely pale all of a sudden. Was it what I had said?

"You know the song?" I asked.

"Mads loved it," the sister replied. "He was a big Liverpool fan."

"I see."

I sensed the tension in the room grow. I wasn't going to get any more out of these people.

"I should go," I said.

"You should," the mother moaned.

I thanked them both for their time, then left the room feeling strange. I had no idea what was up and down in this case. Morten approached me as I came out.

"So what did they say?" he asked.

"Not much. It was more what they didn't say that interested me. I think they're lying. They know something. Something very important."

"Mrs. Frost!"

I turned and saw Doctor Faaborg coming towards me with a smile. "Mrs. Frost, I have to speak to you."

"Hello doctor," I said. "This is Morten, my boyfriend."

"Well, hello there. You're a very lucky fellow. I hope you realize that," Doctor Faaborg said with a grin. "To be the guy that goes home with the great Emma Frost."

"I am and I do," Morten said while they shook hands.

"So what did you want to tell me?" I asked, trying to drown the blush on my cheeks. I never could get used to people seeing me as this big author. It was just me. I was just Emma.

"Well, it is very interesting, in fact. After we spoke last time, I decided to ask about it at our staff meeting this afternoon and you were absolutely right."

"Right about what?"

"About the injection, of course. No one made any injection into Mads Schou's thigh. So the injection-wound in his thigh has to be older. He must have had it when he arrived."

40

APRIL 2012

"WHERE ARE WE GOING, SIGNE?"

Signe was driving the rented scooter up the mountain while Mads was clinging on to her back. The wind was warm in their faces, the city full of lights behind them. In front of them were enthroned the biggest mansions in all of Monaco.

"Signe I'm not sure...Please just tell me what we're doing. I don't want to get into more trouble, I...I really should..."

"Don't be such a wimp," she hissed, sounding awfully a lot like her dad had towards her when she was a child. "You know you want to do this. You know you're going to like it."

"Signe I don't think..."

"Shut up Mads! Just shut up and do as I tell you. You'll thank me later. I'm getting us out of this mess. You don't have a choice. I'm doing this with or without you."

They reached a road and she took a turn sharply. Mads held on to her waist so he wouldn't fall off. Signe stopped the engine and they both got off the scooter. She looked at Mads who, like her, had his face hidden behind his helmet. She closed his visor so she couldn't see his eyes. "There you go.

No one will ever recognize you, in case they have cameras on the wall," she said with a smile and then closed her own.

"What are we doing?" Mads asked. She could hear he was getting anxious.

"We're getting the money," she said. "Come with me."

She walked down the road along a tall brick wall, then stopped. "This is perfect," she said. She walked along the wall then jumped up and grabbed ahold of the edge, then pulled her body over. Mads followed her closely. They ran towards the house.

"Who lives here?" Mads asked.

She shrugged. "I don't know. But I bet they're rich, don't you?"

"So you're going to steal their money?"

"No. We're going to steal their money." Signe sat down in the grass underneath a window. She pulled out a small bag from her pocket. "Here," she said and handed him one of the small colorful pills from inside the bag. "Take it."

"What is it?" Mads whispered.

"I don't know." She took hers and swallowed.

"Where did you get it from?"

"Some guy at the casino last night. He offered them to me outside the bathroom. I told him I'd suck his dick if he gave them to me for free."

"You did what?"

"Relax. I didn't do it. I took him into the bathroom then knocked him out with a vase and stole all he had. Take it. It'll make you feel great. Like you can conquer the world."

Signe pushed his hands towards his mouth. Why was he all of a sudden being this way again? She leaned over and whispered:

"Listen. Just follow my lead, okay? Just do what I tell you to."

Mads was staring at her through the helmet. She sensed his eyes on hers. Tired of waiting, she took the pill out of his hand, opened the visor and put it inside his mouth. "Now swallow," she said. To her satisfaction, he obeyed. "Now we wait," she said. "Five minutes, the man told me. Five minutes it takes for the drug to reach your blood stream."

"Then what?" Mads asked.

"Then we attack. Quickly in and quickly out. Don't be scared, Mads. It's easy. Easy as one, two, three."

41

APRIL 2014

Morten and I slept better that night. I was exhausted beyond anything and, to my surprise, I fell asleep as soon as my head hit the pillow. I woke up a couple of times gasping and calling out Maya's name until I realized where I was, in the darkness of a hotel room.

The next morning I felt a little better. Sleep was just what I needed, even if my dreams really worried me. I kept seeing Maya in a dark room all alone crying asking me to come and help her. It had been the same dream every night, but this time there was a twist to it. This time, Victor had been there as well. He had been sitting in the corner with a rat in his hand, gently petting it and telling me how much he loved rats. While we ate breakfast, I kept wondering why he had said that on the phone. He had told me he liked rats. He had never said anything like that before and, knowing him, nothing was coincidental. There was something about rats that he wanted me to know. But what and why?

"Are you alright?" Morten asked.

"Yes. I'm sorry. A little distracted, why?"

"You haven't touched your food yet and I'm almost done. It's very unlike you. Are you thinking about yesterday?"

"That came up as well, yes," I said and drank my orange juice. "I keep wondering if it could be the mother who wanted to get the son out of the picture. Maybe to make sure he didn't inherit the money. You should have heard them. They practically said he was a disgrace because he wanted to divorce his wife."

"A little drastic to want him killed because of that, don't you think?" Morten asked with a cute smile.

He was right. Even for a rich upper-class family like this, it was a little drastic. I felt so frustrated once again. I still had no idea who the mysterious woman was or where Signe Schou could be.

"So, what are we up to today?" Morten asked.

"I thought I'd be paying a little surprise visit to Signe Schou's mother. I think I'll take Rebekka with me. No offense, but given her history with her husband and all, I don't think she trusts men very much. I'm not taking any chances. I want the truth from her this time."

"Great. I'll hang out with Sune then," Morten said, annoyed.

"You don't like Sune?" I asked, startled. I loved the guy.

"He's trouble, Emma. I can't stand turning a blind eye and pretending I don't see him breaking the law again and again. It's very uncomfortable for me."

"I know it's hard, but please just do it for me, will you?"

I grabbed Morten's hand. I missed being close to him, but it was just so difficult with everything that was going on. All I could think about was Maya. I was sick to my stomach from worry.

"You don't have to like him," I said. "I didn't like Rebekka much in the beginning either. She is very different from me. Especially her choices. I still find it hard to understand why she has chosen to leave her baby at home with her dad in order to go to work."

Morten frowned. "I completely get that. He's more than a year, Emma. She has to get back at some point if she doesn't want to lose her job," Morten said. "Most people put their children in daycare at that age. At least she has her dad taking care of him."

"I guess so. I didn't work until my kids were four, though."

"And what kind of jobs did you get by then?"

He was right. I was away from the job market for eight years. I couldn't get any job once I decided it was finally time to get one. Everything had changed. I didn't have any education, since I was way too young when I became pregnant, so all I could get was small badly paid jobs until I finally started writing for small magazines. And I had become way too dependent on Michael. Once he dropped the bomb and told me he was in love with someone else and leaving us, I could hardly change a light bulb without his help. It was quite a shock to get back to doing everything on my own.

Morten got up from his chair and wiped his mouth with his napkin. "Shall we go?" he asked.

I looked at my plate. I had hardly eaten anything. I grabbed a croissant and wrapped it in my napkin and took it with me. On our way to the office in the car I checked my phone in the hope that someone could have called... in the desperate hope that Maya had somehow found a phone and tried to call me and I just hadn't heard it, even if I did sleep with it very close to me and checked it several times during the night. But there was nothing. Nothing but old photos of my beautiful daughter that I was suddenly afraid I hadn't appreciated enough while I had her.

If I ever got her back, I was never letting her go again. Not if...*when*, I told myself. When I got her back.

42

APRIL 2014

Signe Schou's mother lived on the small island of Enoe right outside of Karrebaeksminde. We drove there in Rebekka's car. The car was filled with baby toys on the floor and had a blue baby seat in the back. I had forgotten how much having a baby changed everything in your life, including how you lived and the content in your car.

"Just throw that stuff in the back if it bothers you," Rebekka said as I got into the car. The front seat was packed with cracker-boxes, baby-wipes, toys and a garbage bag. I moved it to the backseat and sat down.

"So, I'm guessing it's a boy?" I said and strapped my seatbelt. I had touched something sticky and my fingers felt gross now. I grabbed a tissue from the box and wiped it clean.

"Sorry about that," Rebekka said and drove off down the road. "And yes. You're right. His name is William. Named after Sune's grandfather."

"I love how you guys manage to work together and still be a couple," I said.

Rebekka took a turn while looking like she was thinking about what I had said. "Well, it isn't always easy," she said.

"Oh. But you make it look easy."

She shrugged. "I guess we're doing okay. It's a lot of work, but I guess that's just life, right?"

I was a little startled to hear that they weren't the all-time happy couple that I had taken them for, but once I thought about it, I knew that nobody was. If my divorce had taught me anything, it was that a relationship took all your effort to make it work. There was no room for slacking off; if you for one second became too comfortable and thought everything was running smoothly while you were busy doing other things and not attending to how your relationship was doing, then *snap*, it could be over. All it took was ten seconds. Ten seconds where he came to you one afternoon while you were sitting by the computer and told you that you two needed to talk. I still remembered it as one of the most terrifying moments of my life. There I was in my own little world of contentment, not realizing that a few seconds later, my entire world would be ripped apart. The worst part was his coldness when I started pleading with him to stay. I hated that part and regretted it every second of my life. Me crying my eyes out, begging him not to leave and him just starting to pack without a word, without so much as looking in my direction.

Today, I was glad we split up and, looking back, I'd only been fooling myself. We weren't happy. I hadn't been happy at all in that marriage. But it took distance and time to realize that. It was brutal on the children, but in the end, it was best for all of us. Even if I never could forgive him, I guess I in time learned to accept it...accept the fact that he loved someone else. But I hated the fact that I still felt like I hadn't been good enough for him, that he never thought I was good enough.

"I guess you're right," I said.

"And you and Morten? You seem like a great couple," she said and drove onto the bridge leading to Enoe Island.

"We are. He's the most supportive and loving man I have ever been with. He's amazing, really. He loves my kids and I can't believe how sweet he always is. Sometimes I feel like he's from another planet. I've never met a guy quite like him," I said and looked out at the ocean underneath us. The sun had been shining all morning and it made the ocean sparkle. It was gorgeous.

"But...?" Rebekka said.

I looked at her. What did she mean by that? "Excuse me?"

"I sense there is a but in there somewhere," she said.

I shook my head. That was a strange thing to say, I thought. I didn't like it. Of course Morten and I had fights, yes, but all couples had that. It was very rare, though.

But that's not what it is, is it? You know there is a but in there. You know you have your doubts about him. You know you've thought about it too, but won't admit it to yourself. Because from the outside, he is perfect and you keep telling yourself that he is, but there is something missing. There is something vital missing from your relationship and you know it. Rebekka sees it. She knows.

"I don't know," I said as Rebekka drove into a driveway and stopped the car. "I guess all couples have their issues, you know?"

Rebekka nodded. "Guess so."

I felt like she saw right through me. What was this feeling all of a sudden? Was I really having doubts about Morten? I guess I was. He was sweet and perfect and all, but I wasn't exactly getting what I needed from him. The thought made me feel awful. I loved him, I really did, but where was the passion? He hadn't exactly swept me off my feet. I knew he loved me and showed me in his actions, but we were supposed to be in love, we were supposed to be all over each other and we weren't. Not just because of Maya being gone, no it had been going on long before that. The passion simply wasn't there and I needed it. I needed it badly. I shook the thought. I was just being ridiculous. Morten was perfect. End of story.

"Let's go knock on the door," Rebekka said and got out.

I followed her and looked at the big old white villa in front of us with views over the ocean. I was quite surprised that Signe Schou's mother could afford to live in a place like this. Wasn't she supposed to be poor?

43

APRIL 2014

Mads was anxious. They had been doing all kinds of tests on him all morning. He was trying to move his pinky again and again and he knew they saw it, but he was afraid they wouldn't realize that he did it deliberately.

All night, he had been awake inside of his darkness recalling pictures of his life, trying to stick to the happy wonderful days and not all the bad ones.

Signe had been the love of his life, but the more he thought about her and their marriage, the more he realized that he might not have been in love with her as much as he was in love with what she represented. At least not in the beginning.

They had only seen each other for a week before he had presented her to his mother. Today, he knew that it wasn't because he was so head over heels in love with her that he just needed to show her off to his family, like he had told her he was. No, he had another reason; he had a completely different agenda.

Signe was the complete opposite of his mother. She came from a poor very broken family, she dressed provocatively and she had short boyish hair. She was what his mother would call bad company, a rebel, and Mads loved that about her. She was nothing like the kind of woman his mother wanted him to marry.

So, he fell in love. He adored her despite her many tantrums and strange desires that led to very destructive behavior...behavior that would end up terminating his love for her once he realized just how dangerous she really was.

But how could he have known? How could he have foreseen what was going to happen to them? He had been blinded by his love for her and the love of the life they had together. The adventurous side to her was different. He had never encountered anything like it before. It was thrilling and exciting, until the day it went overboard. Oh, the many times he had regretted not having left her the first time. It could have been so easy for him to just leave her there in Egypt when she had started flirting with the bartender. He never understood why he didn't. But a part of him had felt intrigued. Aroused even. He wanted to see how far she was going to take it, how far she would go. And then, much to his surprise, she had gone all the way. She had walked into the restroom with that guy and let him touch her, let him...oh, how he had felt bad in those seconds after the door had closed. How brutal it had been to sit out there in the bar and picture what she was doing with him in there. That was when all sense and sensibility inside of him had been replaced with anger. Furious anger so deep he was ready to kill for it. The jealousy had felt so overpowering, there was nothing else he could do. Mads had hit the bartender so hard he had smashed his head on the porcelain sink. And it had felt so good. He had felt so good punching him. So incredible powerful...for the first time in his life.

But after that, it was too late. There was no turning back for him. He had killed a guy and the two of them were suddenly accomplices. They were freaking Bonnie and Clyde all of a sudden and Mads couldn't say he hadn't enjoyed it. A big part of him had. But he had also realized the consequences and Signe hadn't. She had kept going and, even if every sensible part of him screamed to get the hell out of this marriage, he had followed her. He had let her do those awful things and put them in very dangerous situations. Why? He didn't really have an explanation. He loved the thrill more than he loved the life that was waiting for him back home.

But that was all over now. Now he had finally come to his senses. Her magic spell had lost its touch on him after what happened in Monaco. After that, he finally realized just how crazy she was, how dangerous it was for him to be with her. But he had to admit, he had felt alive with her. Those weeks they were travelling together, he had felt more alive than ever in his life at home in the big mansion with his wealthy family.

But he had also known Signe would end up being the death of him one day. And he was right.

"I'm afraid that it is as I suspected," he heard the man he knew was his doctor say.

"There's no brain activity?" he heard his sister ask.

A small whimper from his mother followed.

"No. What we see here, the tiny movements in the tip of his finger are nothing more than reflex muscle jerks. I'm sorry."

No! No! I'm here. People I'm here. How can this happen? How can they not know I'm alive in here? How can their instruments not detect that I do have brain activity? That I am thinking? HEEEEELP!!!

The room was suddenly filled with a loud high-pitched sound that Mads guessed was coming from the monitors in the room. Shoes moved across the room, then stopped.

"Wait a minute," the doctor suddenly said.

"What is it?" Thilde asked.

"I have never...This isn't possible...Nurse! Come in here!"

44

APRIL 2014

Signe Schou's mother was what I would call a big woman. She was tall and had very broad shoulders. On the door, it said *Susssanne Bo*. Rebekka introduced herself and told her they had spoken on the phone. The mother nodded.

"Ah yes, the reporter. I remember. I don't have any more to say, I still don't know where Signe is," she said. "As I told you on the phone, I haven't seen her since her wedding."

"I understand that," Rebekka said. "But we have a few more questions that I would like to ask you, if that's okay?"

Susssanne Bo looked perplexed. "I really don't think there's any need to...," she paused and looked like she had gotten a good idea. "Well okay, but what's in it for me?"

"What do you mean?" Rebekka asked.

"It's going to cost you."

"What?" Rebekka asked. She looked at me with an expression that said she thought the woman had lost it.

I found my wallet and pulled out five hundred kroner. I handed it to her. "Here you go. Now will you talk to us?"

Susssanne Bo grinned and opened the door. "Come on in. Five hundred kroner will give you half an hour. After that, I'll ask for a thousand."

"What's with your name?" I asked, as we walked inside and sat at her dining room table. I was quite startled by the views from the house. I didn't understand how she could live like this after all I had heard about Signe's background. Had the mother remarried?

"What's that dear?" she asked and sat down.

"Why do you spell your name with three 's's?" I asked.

Rebekka put her phone on the table. "I'm recording the conversation," she said. "Just to let you know."

"Fine by me," the mother said. "And to answer your question, I changed my name some years ago. This name fits me better. Numerologically speaking, it's a much better combination for me. It's more compatible with my birth-number. The 's' adds more ones to my life and I need that."

I stared at the woman for a little while, wondering what she had just said. I knew nothing about numerology, but had always wondered about the name changing thing. I wasn't closer to understanding it. But she looked like she had just told me the deepest insight to this world.

"I see," I said, hoping she wouldn't say more.

"Tell me about your daughter," Rebekka said.

Susssanne Bo chuckled. "What's there to tell? She's a troublemaker; she married a rich man and now I don't have to take care of her anymore or worry if she gets herself into more trouble. She's someone else's problem now."

"You say she's a troublemaker, how's that?" Rebekka asked.

"As a child, she would always get herself into trouble. You know, fights, stealing from stores, being expelled from school. Stuff like that. She was born like that. Born to be wild. Her father's child."

"And her father is in prison now?" I asked and spotted crystals on the dresser behind her.

"Yes. And they can keep him there for all I care."

I detected a deep anger when she talked about him. I wondered if her profound hurt from what happened with him had made her resent Signe. Maybe that was why she was so busy getting her married well.

"So you say you haven't seen your daughter since April 2012?" Rebekka asked.

"That's correct. She got married and went off on her honeymoon. I never saw her after that."

"So, don't you worry that she is alright?" I asked, startled. How could a mother not worry? I worried constantly about my children. Even when I knew they were just in school. Even when they were sitting right next to me.

"Not really."

"They haven't seen her at the hospital where her husband is lying in a coma. Don't you worry that something might have happened to her as well?"

"No."

Her coldness was terrifying. I couldn't believe her.

"You do know that her marriage didn't work out, don't you?" I asked.

"I don't really care," she said. "Signe is a big girl."

"I spoke to her husband's family, his sister to be precise. She told me she was certain Signe went back to live with you when they came back from their honeymoon and they split up," I said.

"Well, that's not true."

I looked at Susssanne Bo for a long time to try to detect if she was lying. I was usually very good and spotting a liar, but there was nothing on her face indicating she was one. Yet there was something that simply didn't add up.

"Have you remarried?" I asked.

The woman laughed. "No. I'm not falling into that trap again."

I found that to be very strange. How on earth could she afford to live like this?

"So, what do you do for a living?"

Susssanne Bo chuckled. "I don't."

"Excuse me?"

"I don't do anything for a living. Now, if you'll excuse me...your time is up."

I looked at the clock on the wall. We had only been there ten minutes.

There was something in what I had asked her that made her want us to leave. I was on to something here.

"Could I use your bathroom before we leave?" Rebekka suddenly asked.

"Of course. There is one right next to the kitchen down the hall," Susssanne Bo answered.

Rebekka left and I was now alone with this woman and all her crystals on the counters everywhere.

"So you're that author, aren't you?" she asked. "You're Emma Frost?"

"Yes I am."

"So will this be a book? Will you write about me?" she asked with a grin. "'Cause it might cost you."

I felt appalled by the woman's greed. "Well, I probably won't. I'm just looking for my daughter. She drove the car that hit Mads Schou and I'm trying to figure out what happened to her afterwards."

"Ouch. She's the runaway? That sounds more like something Signe would do. Well, you think you know them, huh?"

I had to really restrain myself from yelling at this woman. I wanted to tell her my daughter was nothing like that. Nothing at all. Luckily, Rebekka returned.

"Let's go," she said. "I think we have what we need."

I got up and we started walking towards the entrance when Rebekka suddenly stopped and turned to look at the woman. "Oh, by the way...who have you had locked up in the basement?"

Susssanne Bo went pale. Her mouth turned downwards. "Excuse me?"

"I was just wondering. There was a huge lock on the door from the kitchen to the basement so I walked down there to have a look and found a bed and some clothes in a closet. So I was just wondering who's been living down there with the door locked?"

Susssanne Bo seemed perplexed. She was about to lose it now. I was afraid she would try to hurt us, but the anger soon dampened and sadness replaced it. Suddenly, she changed her expression. Tears were in her eyes. I was now standing in front of a real human being.

"You kept her down there, didn't you?" Rebekka asked. "You locked her up when she returned from her honeymoon. Why?"

Susssanne Bo's voice shivered as she spoke. "To keep her out of trouble. She had completely lost it. It was for her own good."

I shook my head. "I don't believe you. I think Mads' family paid you to keep her away from him. Am I right? How else could you afford a house like this? They gave you this house to keep her locked up in, didn't they? How else could you afford to live in it without working?"

Susssanne Bo didn't say anything. She didn't have to. Her silence confirmed my theory. The woman was beyond greedy.

"I wasn't being a monster. I didn't treat her like a prisoner. I let her have contact with the world. I gave her a laptop and fed her well every day."

I looked at Susssanne's arm and spotted two large purple bruises. "But she escaped, didn't she? How did she escape? Is that how you got those bruises?"

Susssanne looked down at her arm and rolled up the sleeve so we could see. It looked really bad. "Somehow, she got ahold of an iron bar from the basement. I don't know how...she attacked me with it. I haven't seen her since. That's the truth."

"How long ago was this?" Rebekka asked.

"It was on Saturday the 19th. The day the accident happened to Mads. I am so afraid she had something to do with it. You have no idea what she is capable of."

45

APRIL 2012

They could hear children's screams and voices of joy when they approached the front door of the mansion. Signe grabbed Mads' hand as they took off their helmets and rang the doorbell.

"Let me do the talking," she whispered.

Her pulse was loud and roaring in her ears. The drugs had started working and she sensed nothing, no fear anymore, just thrill and excitement. She felt like all her senses were intensified. Like she could hear every insect in the bushes, see every light in the darkness of the night.

"Shouldn't the kids be in bed?" Mads whispered anxiously. She looked into his eyes. He was wearing a blissful smile. The drugs were doing the trick and, in a few moments, he wouldn't care about the kids anymore.

There was movement behind the door and it opened. A man appeared. He looked angry. "Who are you? What are you doing here?" he asked. "How did you get past the gate?"

Signe giggled. "We climbed the wall," she said. "Right down there by the end of your yard."

"You did what?" The man's face was turning red.

Mads and Signe both giggled.

"I'm calling the police," he said.

"We have something for you," Signe said.

The man looked strangely at them. "You have something for me? What is that supposed to mean?"

"It means we have something we need to give to you," Mads said. "It's urgent."

Signe could tell the man liked Mads. He didn't look like someone who would ever do anything bad, he was one of them, he was wealthy like him. The man could somehow see that, or maybe they could smell it on one another. Signe didn't know, but she had been around wealthy people long enough to know that they always knew who was one of them and who wasn't.

"So, what is it?" The man asked impatiently.

Signe looked at him with her eyes heavy with mascara and eyeliner. She had painted them almost black. She liked to think of it as war-paint. She knew he was confused by her, so she let Mads take over. The man stared at Signe's cleavage. She liked it. She liked that he was watching her, devouring her with his eyes.

"He has it," she said and pointed at Mads.

"It's in my pocket." Mads reached down and the man turned to have a look. That was when Signe pulled out a small rubber baton that she had bought to be able to defend herself. She hit him on the back of his head and the man sank to the ground with a loud thud. Her leather gloves were squeaking as she put the baton back inside of her jacket and signaled Mads to enter.

They could hear the children screaming with joy even louder as they snuck inside, making as little noise as possible. Signe felt the joyful thrill once again and enjoyed the moment. This was what she lived for. This was worth losing all the money, just to get to experience this ecstasy again.

They dragged the man inside by pulling his legs and closed the door gently after them. They sneaked through the hallway, across a living room till they reached the entrance to an indoor-pool area. Two young girls were in the water splashing at each other and screaming, while a woman was sitting in a chair reading her book with a glass of red wine on the table in front of her.

Signe watched them with an odd feeling inside of her. She couldn't put words to it; she didn't know what it was, she only knew that she hated these girls instantaneously. She hated this family more than anything in this world. She loathed them and their happiness and their family life. A life she had once known and lived, until the day when it was suddenly taken away. Until the day when her dad, for the first time, entered her room one night and showed her how much he really loved her. Until the day he showed her how painful real love was.

That was when everything changed and she had tried all of her childhood to get the happiness and the family life back...desperately tried to mend the broken pieces and make her parents happy again. She had thought she was somehow to blame for things changing. She had thought it was her duty to fix it again and desperately tried to for years and years. Until the day when they came for him. Until the day when the police knocked on their door and took her dad away and doctors and teachers tried to make her understand that her father was a sick scumbag and his love for her was wrong.

Staring at the happy faces playing in the water tricked something inside of her. It opened a door she hadn't dared to open before. With the drugs rushing in her veins, she suddenly felt an urge to show these young girls that happiness like this was an illusion. It would always be taken away at some point. The world was unfair and they might as well learn that now.

46

APRIL 2014

"So let me get this straight," Morten said.

We had come back to the office where he and Sune were sitting at the computer, going through the profiles of each of the women who said they would attend the party's profiles for the third time, to see if anything came up as important.

"She kept her daughter locked up in her basement because Mads Schou's family paid her to?"

"That's what she basically told us," I said, and sat down in front of Rebekka's computer.

"Basically?" Morten asked. "You mean to say she didn't say it, but you just concluded it or what?"

"Well, she didn't deny it," I said. "And she did admit to having locked up the girl since they came back from their honeymoon."

"Wow," Morten exclaimed.

"I know. It's really sick," I said and turned on the computer.

"But you can't just conclude that she was paid to do it," Morten said using his professional police voice. I hated when he did that. When he tried to teach me how to work like a real policeman. I wasn't one and I was never going to be.

"You need to get your facts straight. You need proof," he said.

"Yeah. You don't really know that she did it for money," Sune continued. "Not for sure, that is."

So apparently, the boys were ganging up on us now.

"No, but you should have seen the house she was living in," Rebekka said and grabbed a chair next to me.

I tapped rapidly on the keyboard. Rebekka looked at me. "I swear it's just like looking at Sune," she said. "He does the same thing with the fingers. It's creepy. You're just like him."

I shrugged and continued. Sune and Morten looked at me from their desk.

"What are you doing?" Morten asked and got up from his chair. He came closer and looked over my shoulder.

I kept my fingers running across the keyboard.

"What are you doing, Emma?" Morten asked again.

"Just getting my facts straight," I said and hit a key. Numbers rolled across the screen.

"No you didn't," Morten said. "Tell me you didn't just hack yourself into her account? Oh my God, I'm going to lose my badge over this, aren't I?"

I chuckled and scrolled through the numbers from two years ago. Then I stopped. "Here it is. See, here and here." I pointed at the numbers. There was no doubt. Huge transfers of millions of kroner several times during the second part of 2012. The money came from a company called Lundbit.

"I think I want to marry you," Sune said.

Rebekka laughed.

I ignored them. We were onto something big here and I was really excited. "Lundbit is Mads Schou's family business, right? I asked. "You said so the other day, Rebekka."

"That's true," she replied.

I leaned back in the chair. "I'll be damned. There's your proof."

Morten shook his head and looked at me. "What am I going to do with you? You're going to cost me my job."

"As long as it brings my daughter back somehow, I don't mind," I said. "I just don't quite see how it will, yet. But we're getting closer. I can feel it."

Just as I said the words, my phone rang. I picked it up. It was doctor Faaborg.

"Emma, darling, I have great news. I thought you'd like to know that we have detected brain activity in Mads Schou."

"Brain activity?"

Darling?

"Yes. We don't know much yet, but his brain is definitely working."

I almost dropped the phone. Brain activity meant he was alive, it meant there was hope for him. It also meant he wasn't going to die and that meant my daughter wouldn't be accused of murder. This news meant the world to me. Finally, things seemed to be shaping up for us. Finally.

47

APRIL 2014

M ads was filled with such a profound relief. They had seen him. They knew he was in here and that he wasn't brain dead. He would have laughed with joy and let tears roll across his cheeks, if only he could.

Voices were blending in the room. Lots of voices, most of which he had never heard before. They were agitated. Among them, he could hear the doctor. The doctor had sent Mads' mother and sister to stand by Mads and talk to him.

"It helps to hear familiar voices," he said.

So now they were holding his hands and talking to him while nurses and doctors were chatting in the background. It all blended in and confused him slightly. He tried to squeeze his mother's hand, but didn't succeed. Then he went back to moving the tip of the pinky and his mother soon saw it.

"He really is alive," she gasped and called for the doctor to see it. "I think he's trying to speak to us."

"It might still only be reflexes," the doctor said, "but keep talking to him and see if he reacts."

Mads kept moving his finger trying to let them know he could hear everything they said and several hours passed like this. Still, they didn't understand what he was telling them. Mads felt helpless and frustrated and soon grew very very tired. He guessed it was getting late in the day when his sister leaned over and spoke in his ear.

"Mads. I have to get Mom home and get something to eat and then some rest. She needs it. We'll be back tomorrow morning."

Mads felt like crying. All this time he had tried to communicate with them and still they hadn't understood. For some reason, it made him panic even worse than when they didn't know he was alive. The thought was claustrophobic.

What if they never get me out of this condition? What if I have to stay like this, trapped in here, for the rest of my life?

Never had he felt lonelier than in the seconds when he heard the footsteps disappear and the room suddenly go dreadfully quiet. All the voices were gone and all he could hear were the machines helping him breathe.

Where did everybody go?

Mads sobbed inside of his mind and felt sorry for himself. He had no idea what time it was or how long it would take before his loneliness would once again be broken, but he knew that it would take a long time. Too long a time. It always did. The nights always felt endless. A nurse would check on him later in the evening, before nighttime came, but that was it. That was all the company he would get. It felt like an eternity ahead of him. An eternity of loneliness.

But at least they now know you're not brain dead. At least they know you're alive, he tried to cheer himself up. It helped, but only slightly. Hope was such a treacherous companion, wasn't it? Now that he had it, there was always the possibility of being disappointed. Of being let down. There was a new fear that had snuck up on him, the fear of being so close, but never really getting back to life again...the fear that this was all he got.

Mads thought about Signe and how angry he still was at her for what she had done that night in Monaco. He remembered the second he realized that she had finally lost it. That it was no longer a game. It was the look in her eyes when she saw those girls playing in the pool. After that, he knew there was no turning back. What she did was so horrifying, he could no longer love her. It was simply impossible. He knew he had to get away from her. Once he escaped from the house, he had called his mom and asked for her help. He still remembered the feeling of utter terror inside of him when he had told her everything. He was crying on the phone when he begged her to get her away from him, to take him back, to give him his life back as he knew it before he met Signe.

"You're not getting a divorce," she had said. "That is out of the question. We don't get divorces in our family. But we can get rid of her. Make sure she disappears. Stay where you are son. I'll take care of everything."

Mads knew it was cowardly of him, but he accepted the deal. Even if it meant he had to become what he had always feared. Even if it meant going back to being one of them, working for his dad's pharmaceutical company making money off other's misery. But he had no idea where else to turn. His mother could take care of everything. She could make all the bad things go away like she always had. Even this.

Why did you have to do this? Mads cried inside of his darkness. *We could have had such a wonderful life. Why did you have to go crazy like this? Don't tell me it was the drugs. Don't say that it was, 'cause it wasn't. It was something else. It was the beast inside of you that you could no longer control. I knew it when I married you. I knew it was there. It was part of the reason I married you in the first place. Because I felt drawn to the beast, but I never realized the consequences. Not before it was too late.*

Mads was busy feeling sorry for himself, when suddenly, he heard the door to his room open and steps approaching. Then he stopped sobbing and smiled on the inside. He knew the sound of those shoes.

48

APRIL 2014

I was glad to realize that Mads Schou was alone in his hospital room when I entered. I was afraid he would be surrounded by nurses and doctors. That was why I had chosen to wait to stop by till the evening. I had sent Morten back to the hotel to rest and call his daughter, who had left a message on his machine, telling him she thought he was spending too much time with me and that he should come home.

I walked inside and placed my bouquet of flowers on the table next to him. I felt a pinch in my stomach as I walked closer. He didn't look any different, but I saw him differently now that I knew his brain was working. That was why I had come. I had to see him for myself. I had to see the difference, even if there was none. In my mind, everything had changed. The doctor had told me he wasn't certain this meant Mads would actually wake up, but it meant that now there was a possibility that he would. Someday.

To me, that was a huge difference.

I stood next to him and looked at his pale badly bruised face. I felt a lump in my throat thinking about Maya driving the car that hit him and made those bruises. I thought about how awful it must have been for her to experience this, to think that she might have killed someone.

"Hi Mads," I said, feeling stupid, since I knew he couldn't answer. But he could hear me, couldn't he? I believed he heard everything. I was certain he did. Somehow, I had always sensed he did.

I cleared my throat. The lump of tears was growing bigger and threatening to burst. It was like all the last days' frustration and worry decided to come to the surface all at once in this moment. I felt like crying so badly, but held it back the best I could. A few tears rolled across my cheek and I wiped them away with the back of my hand. A few more escaped and I decided to let them.

"I'm so sorry," I said. Then I laughed at myself. "I'm getting ahead of myself here. You don't even know who I am." I grabbed his hand and held it in mine. I looked at it while I spoke. "I'm the mother of the girl who drove into you with her car."

Speaking of Maya made me cry harder and soon, I couldn't hold it back any longer. I was holding his hand while my tears fell on it and wet his fingers.

"I...I...you know...I know she would have been here herself if she could, but somehow she can't...and I...we don't know...The thing is, I can't find her. She's vanished and we have no idea where she is. Oh my God, I wish you were awake and could tell me who it was that pushed you in front of her car. I don't know what I expected, but when Doctor Faaborg called, I somehow expected you to be able to communicate with me. I felt hope, you know? I mean, I was first of all thrilled to know that you weren't dead, that you were alive, but...I don't know. I'm just being silly here. I just want to make sure you know that Maya is sorry. I know she is. I just know it."

I was crying heavily now and let go of Mads' hand. I walked to the sink and grabbed some paper towels. I wiped my nose and face and looked at myself in the small mirror, wiping away the black make-up under my eyes. That was when I saw it. In the reflection of the mirror, I saw him move his finger again. I gasped and turned to look. His pinky was still moving and, suddenly, I realized that there was a rhythm to it. It wasn't just random movement. It seemed to be in a pace, maybe even a beat.

Why hadn't I seen this before?

I walked back towards him while looking at his pinky. I reached into my purse and found a piece of paper and started writing it down.

"Short, long, short, short, long," I mumbled while writing. Could it really be? Was he really communicating with me?

I kept writing down dots and dashes until it started repeating itself. I looked at it when suddenly it occurred to me how to read it.

I leaned over and gave Mads Schou a gentle kiss on the cheek. "Thank you," I whispered. "Thank you so much."

49

APRIL 2012

S he was dreaming. At least she thought she was. Maybe it was more like a picture or a movie inside of her head that wouldn't go away. In the dream, she saw a mother hen with her two little chicks. She didn't want to have this dream, but it wouldn't go away. Signe tried to think about something else, but couldn't. All she saw was the mother hen running around in circles, headless, with blood spurting out of its neck. Then those two small chickens covering their faces with their wings, running around screaming and being splashed with the blood from the mother...their yellow feathers turning red from the blood.

Signe couldn't remember what happened after that, she told the officer in English. She had no idea how she had ended up in the street where they found her, smeared in blood.

"You say you were with someone in the house?" the officer asked.

"I think my husband was there as well. I don't know. It was all a dream," she answered. "I don't know why you're keeping me here over a dream."

One of the two officers leaned over. His breath smelled bad, Signe thought. He had something stuck on his chin. Was it food? She couldn't tell. She was wondering when she would get out of here. And where was Mads? She couldn't remember. The last thing she did remember was them driving on a scooter, but she had no idea where they were going. All she could remember were those bloody chickens and their awful screams.

"A woman was killed in her house yesterday and you were found smeared in blood in the street outside of their house. Her husband gave us a description matching you and your husband perfectly. He told us you two rang their doorbell and then knocked him down. Now, where is your husband?"

"A woman was killed? I don't...I don't understand."

The officer looked at her seriously. He put a bag of pills on the table. "We found these in your pocket."

Signe looked at the clear plastic bag and recognized the pills. But she didn't tell the officer. Instead, she lied. "I have no idea where those came from."

The officer slammed his fist into the desk. Signe jumped.

"Don't lie to us, young lady. This is very serious. The woman's head was cut off, goddammit. Cut off with an axe. The children watched as you swung the axe at her and her head rolled into the swimming pool."

Signe tried to understand what the man was telling her, but all she could think of was chickens. And blood. A lot of blood. She didn't understand what he was trying to get her to do. She looked down at her own clothes and realized they were smeared in blood. As a matter of fact, there was blood everywhere. It was running down the walls in thick stripes. It was splashing on the floor; it was even in the faces of the two officers who were now yelling at her. Signe gasped and whimpered as the blood on the floor became a flood and soon covered everything. She crawled up on the chair so her feet wouldn't touch it. The officers were yelling and telling her to sit down. Her hands were cuffed to the side of the chair so she couldn't get loose from it. Why weren't they afraid? Didn't they understand the blood was rising? They would drown. She would drown if they didn't free her. Signe tried to tell them. She tried to yell at them that there was blood everywhere, but they didn't seem to understand. They kept asking the same question over and over again.

"Where is your husband? Where is your husband?"

"Please," she pleaded and pulled her cuffed hands till they started bleeding. She tried to move the chair, but it was bolted to the floor.

"Please let me free. I'm drowning. I'm going to DIE here!"

The blood was coming closer and closer now and now reaching her waist. She tried to stand up in the chair, but couldn't stand up straight because of her hands. The blood was now at her neck and soon would be in her mouth. The officer's questions were drowned out by the blood in their mouths. It was spurting and spluttering out of them as they spoke. Signe whimpered and screamed as the blood filled her lungs and she was slowly forced to stop breathing.

50

APRIL 2014

The numerologist looked at Mads Schou in his hospital bed. He was breathing steadily with the help of the machines. His eyes were closed and he looked like he was sleeping soundly.

But she knew he wasn't. She knew he was awake and could hear everything. She had seen it the first time when she was in his room. She had seen him move the tip of his pinky as if to signal to her and she knew he was somehow trying to communicate. But she had also known that she was the only one who knew and, as long as the doctors believed Mads was brain dead, then it was no use telling them he wasn't, right? After all, what better punishment than to have him buried alive? To have him forever regret his actions ten feet under. After all, she had offered him a new start to life, a new beginning, but he had refused. He had tried to escape. There was nothing else she could do for him. She hadn't been able to inject the medicine properly in his leg on the day of the party. The plan had backfired and he had run away. So, she had to push him out in front of that car, hadn't she? She just had to do it. She had no regrets.

But now, she had heard that they knew. Somehow, they had come to know that he was alive, so she had to do something. She couldn't have him waking up and then tell everyone what he knew. Of course she couldn't allow that to happen.

It would simply ruin everything.

"I still remember when you came to my office," she said, as she stroked his cheek. "Your mother sent you. She had contacted me and told me to take care of you. She told me you had been through something traumatic and you needed my help. She told me to go ahead and medicate you if necessary. You were so handsome, Mads, when you walked into my office. A little shy and very, very afraid. But we talked for hours, remember? We met three times a week for almost two years and, finally one day, you opened up to me and told me everything. You told me everything you had done, you and that awful wife of yours. You told me you couldn't live with yourself and what you had done. And I held your hand and told you I could help you. I could give you a treatment that would make you forget everything. But it meant you had to give up all your memories. And you wouldn't do that. You told me you couldn't. But I wasn't going to let go of you that easily. I knew I could get you and your wife into my program, even if I had to force you into it. You were perfect for it, only you didn't realize it. You told me you didn't know where Signe was, but you did, didn't you?" The numerologist laughed and let one of her long nails scratch Mads' cheek and leave a long mark.

"I even came to you at your house, remember? I told you I wanted you to find Signe for me, that I wanted to help her. But you told me I was insane. I told you it was easy to forget your past. Easy as one, two, three. You remember that? Huh? I held a gun to your face and told you it was so easy and that I wanted to save the both of you, but you overpowered me and grabbed the gun. You told me to stay away from you and never contact you again. But I couldn't, how could I? Oh Mads, I was awake every night. Me and Misty lay awake and talked about how we could get you two to join the program. That was when I came up with the idea of the party. I found Signe on Facebook and realized she was active there. I invited the both of you and many others to a murder party and knew she would want to come. With the way you described her, I knew she couldn't resist. I got the idea from an old Miss Marple mystery. You're probably too young to know it.

But it's quite a good book. I knew if I invited Signe she would come. I knew her murderous nature would make her want to come and make a real murder out of it. It was the perfect setting, wasn't it? She could sweep right in and kill someone there just for the fun of it. Just like you told me during our sessions that she liked to do. She liked the excitement. No one would ever suspect her; everyone would look for the one who arranged the party and find nothing, only anonymous. But I had her figured out. It was all just to lure her out of hiding. Oh well. I guess it all went a little haywire, huh? Silly me. I had planned to give you the injection once the lights went out, then as soon as you became lifeless, I would simply carry you out the back door with me. Piece of cake, really. Signe, I had already taken once she approached the theater. It was really simple. She is already in my treatment program. And she is making such great progress, Mads. You should see her. She's already completely forgotten her murderous nature. She is completely new. See, the thing is, Mads. I've been to prison. I know what it's like in there. It was such a terrifying experience and I'm trying to save you all from having to go there. All of you. But you wouldn't listen, Mads, and now it's too late. I can't save all of you. I just have to face that fact."

The numerologist sighed and looked at the clock on the wall. It was six minutes to eight. Six plus eight was fourteen. One plus four was five. The number of the day was also five. Five was believed to be the number of death. She understood what the universe was telling her.

It was time.

The numerologist leaned over and whispered in Mads' ear while putting a finger on the button on the monitor next to him. "I told you it would be easy," she said. "As easy as one, two..."

Beep.

51

APRIL 2014

I stormed into the hotel room and found Morten on the phone with his daughter. I signaled wildly that I was excited then ran to my laptop and opened it. I found my notepad and looked at what I had written down.

Morten told his daughter he had to go and hung up. "What's going on?" he asked.

"Mads Schou told me something," I said, and opened the Internet on my computer.

Morten came closer. "He was awake? He spoke to you?"

"Well not exactly. More of signaled me...with his pinky."

Morten looked disappointed. "The pinky again? Do you really think that is a signal? It sounds a little out there."

I turned and looked at him. I lifted my notepad and showed him the things I had written. He looked confused.

"What's that?"

"My dad used to sail as a child. He tried to teach me all kinds of things about sailing when I was a child, but I never listened much. I did, however, learn about Morse code."

"Morse code? You think he was using Morse code?" Morten asked.

"Yes. I'm certain he was. I remembered in our research about him that he went to Svendborg to go to school after high school for six months, following a tradition in his family. Right before he got married. His parents probably thought he would forget all about Signe while he was there. But guess what kind of school it was? It was a Maritime College. I figured he would have learned Morse code there, right?"

"I guess he could have," Morten said.

It annoyed me that he wasn't as excited as I was, but I shook the feeling. This was a breakthrough for me and I wanted to focus on that.

"All I have to do is translate this," I mumbled and found a web-page to help me. I started translating one sign after another. It wasn't as easy as I thought, but I quickly got the hang of it. Soon letters appeared, and not long after, a sentence grew out of it. Once I was done, I took my notepad and looked at it.

"Well, I'll be damned," I said.

"What does it say?" Morten asked.

"I'm not quite sure if I got everything right, but as far as I can see, it says *WERDQ has your daughter.*"

I gasped and looked up at Morten. Could this really be? Had I gotten a real breakthrough in finding Maya? But what did it mean? Who was WERDQ?

"Ww...," Morten looked confused. "I can't believe it. You got all that out of that?" he said and pointed at the dots and dashes on my pad.

I shrugged. "Well, I guess. I just hope it's right, but it sounds right, don't you think?"

"Yes. I'm just wondering, who is WERDQ? It doesn't sound like the name of a person, does it?"

"Not really. I'm wondering about it as well," I said with a profound exhale. "What can it be? A nickname maybe?"

"That's a possibility. But a strange one, right?"

"Right. But do you have a better suggestion?"

"A town?" Morten asked.

"How can an entire town have my daughter?"

Morten shook his head. "No you're right. Could it be a street name?"

I looked at it again, while rubbing my temples in frustration. It felt so bad to be this close and still not have the answer. "I don't know. Maybe. I just can't see which one. Maybe if I Google it."

"Try that." Morten grabbed a chair and pulled up next to me. I was so happy to have him here with me and not be alone in all this. So what if I didn't feel like he was my passionate soul mate? He made me feel good.

I typed the name and hit enter. A lot of strange sites came up, all in English. I tried to search Danish sites only. Twenty results. But nothing I could use showed up. I went through all of them, but still nothing. I leaned back in the chair with a frustrated snort. This was extremely maddening... to be this close and still not be able to find her. There had to be a way to figure this out, there simply had to be.

Morten kissed my neck. "Maybe we should get some sleep. If we look at it with fresh eyes tomorrow, then maybe we'll be able to solve it."

"You go ahead. I don't think I can sleep at all," I said.

52

APRIL 2012

Signe was lying on the floor when they came to get her. The door opened to her cell, but she hardly reacted. All she could think about was the blood that kept coming after her and drowning her again and again. Every time she opened her eyes, she saw it. It would run down the walls of her cell or it would come up from the floor, just slowly flooding her cell while she hammered on the door for them to let her out.

Feet came closer and she spotted a set of black shoes next to her. They were stained with blood. A hand grabbed her by the neck and she was lifted up from the cold floor.

"Someone is here to take you home," a voice said. The man who spoke had blood on his face.

Signe didn't care. She tried to keep her eyes closed so she wouldn't see all the blood while they carried her outside and she was put in the back of a black limousine. Signe didn't open her eyes until she heard the door being closed and the car started moving. In front of her in the darkness, she saw her mother-in-law. She was wearing a big hat that covered most of her face until she took it off and Signe could see the black eyes staring at her.

"I have paid a lot of money to get you out, Signe," she said. "You don't have to say anything. Mads told me all I need to know. See, my first instinct told me to leave you in this prison, leave you in your misery, but the thing is, they started asking a lot of questions and threatened to go to the Danish police and talk to them about my son. I can't have that. I can't have my family name smothered in dirt like this. Now, as I understand it, you both had taken a lot of drugs and in that rush killed someone, a mother of two children. Now you have to live with yourself and what you have done and I am not going to help you with that. I will, however, turn you over to your mother and she has promised me that she'll keep you as far away from my family as possible. I expect to never see you again, do you understand? I won't have you contact my son ever again. Now, you'll remain married, but you'll never see each other again. If anyone ever asks us, we'll say you ran off, do you understand? I don't care what happens to you as long as you never contact us again. Do you understand?"

Signe swallowed hard then nodded. "I understand."

The car stopped and the woman looked at Signe once again. "And remember one thing, dearie. I will have you put back in that prison if you ever break your promise."

Then she put on her hat and left the car in such a hurry, Signe never even got to say anything. The car quickly started moving again and drove for almost twenty hours. When it finally came to a halt again, the door was opened and Signe walked outside. Waiting for her on the curb, was her mother.

Signe almost burst into tears when she saw her. For the first time in many weeks, she finally managed to keep her thoughts clear of all the blood.

"Mother...I..."

"Save it," her mother said. "Get inside now."

Signe obeyed and walked inside her mother's new home with a small gasp. It was the sight of a painting on the wall that her mother had taken from the old house and hung in the hallway of the new one, that made her remember. Remembering everything that had taken place in her early years made her shiver in anxiety. Listening to her mother's harsh voice again made her remember everything at once. The footsteps at night, the squeaking door when it opened, the shadows on the wall. The men, the many men, that were brought to see her. Her mother standing outside her room taking their money...her father cheering them on, helping them by holding Signe down. It all came back to her now and she fell to the ground inside the hallway and cried.

"I'm so sorry, mother. I'm so sorry."

Her mother walked up behind her holding a belt in her hand. "It's a little too late for that, dearie," she said, then lifted the belt and swung it and whipped Signe till she couldn't scream anymore. Then she carried Signe down the stairs to the basement and locked the door behind her. Signe cried and screamed helplessly into the night, but just like when she was a child, no one heard her. No one cared. She couldn't blame them, she told herself the same thing she had always told herself as a child—She deserved everything she got.

53

APRIL 2014

It was early in the morning when I woke Morten up. I was shaking his arm when he growled and looked at me.

"It's not an 'e'," I said.

"What's going on?" he asked.

"I think I know what it says," I said and showed him the notepad with my scribbles.

"What what said?" he asked and sat up straight.

"The message that Mads gave to me. I got one of the letters wrong. It's not an 'e'."

Morten looked like he needed a minute to remember what it was all about. He looked cute with his hair all messy like that. I liked it when he wasn't too neat and didn't look too much like a policeman.

"Didn't you sleep at all?" he asked and blinked his eyes.

"Nope. Not one bit. But my head feels clearer than ever. Morten, I know what it said."

"So what is it?"

"It's an 'a'. The 'e' is an 'a'." I showed him the Morse alphabet on my laptop. "See how close the two letters are? An 'a' is one dot and a dash, and an 'e' is simply one dot. I think I got it wrong. So that means it says WARDQ instead of WERDQ."

"Yeah, alright. But what does that mean?" Morten asked. "It still doesn't make sense."

"That's what I thought at first, but if you separate the Q from the rest, then it makes complete sense."

"Let me see. WARD Q?"

I nodded eagerly. "Yes. Ward Q."

"As in prison ward Q?" he asked.

"I haven't figured that part out just yet, but I was thinking more in terms of hospital ward Q."

Morten exhaled. It was getting brighter outside and the day was about to begin. "I think I'm a little too tired for this," he groaned.

"You slept all night," I said, as I threw a pair of pants in his face. "Put these on. We're leaving soon."

"Where are we going?" he asked.

"First, we're getting some breakfast. I'm starving. Then we're going to visit Ward Q in Naestved Hospital. I looked it up online. It's a psychiatric ward. I have a feeling they know where Maya is. If they don't, then we visit the prison."

Morten frowned. "How on earth should they know where Maya is? It makes no sense whatsoever. You don't even know that it is in Naestved Hospital or that it is at any hospital. Why don't we take a time-out here Emma and think this through. After all, it was just a man in a coma moving his finger and you interpreted it to be this message about the psychiatric ward having your daughter. It's getting a little far out there."

I stared at him, not believing my own ears.

After all we've been through, this is when he decided to doubt me and my intuition?

"Just trust me on this, Morten," I said and threw a T-shirt at him as well.

"I wore this yesterday," he grumbled.

"Then pick another one," I said, annoyed. "Just get dressed. I have a feeling today is a great day."

Morten got dressed, even if it was slightly reluctantly. I didn't care. I had found what could be a sign of Emma and I wasn't going to let go of it... not this one...even if it seemed crazy to think the psychiatric ward would know anything about where she could be.

It was all I had and I was clinging to it like my life depended on it.

54

APRIL 2014

The parking lot in front of Naestved Hospital was extraordinarily empty. Usually I had to fight to get a space to park my car, but it was so early in the morning that we could pick and choose.

I parked in front of the main entrance, since I didn't know where Ward Q was and we walked inside to ask a receptionist. She gave us directions and we walked around the main building and found the ward behind it in the farthest corner of the hospital area. It was a small yellow brick building with a black roof.

We walked to the main door and opened it. The doors leading further in were heavily locked. We walked to reception and met a small lady with a very smiling face.

"Yes? Can I help you?"

I looked at Morten. We had decided in the car to use—or misuse—the fact that he was a police officer. He wasn't pleased with it, but I had begged him to do it. Now he showed the woman his badge.

"My name is Officer Bredballe, this here is my partner. We need to speak to whoever is in charge of this ward."

The woman stopped smiling and nodded. "Well, of course, Officer, let me just make a call." She picked up the phone and turned her back to us while speaking into it. "...the police...want to talk to you. Uh huh. A man and a woman. What do I tell them? Okay."

She hung up and looked at us. "The doctor will be able to see you right away. It is early and she hasn't started seeing patients yet, so you're in luck."

"Thank you," Morten said.

The small woman handed us two badges. "This is a secure institution. Our patients here can be dangerous, so you need to sign in and wear these in a visible spot all the time while you're here. You can't walk around unattended. These patients are mentally unstable and you never know what they might do. I'll have a guard show you to the doctor's office. Olav?"

A big guy in a green polo shirt with the hospital's name on it stuck his head out of a door behind her. "Yes?"

"These two need to be shown to the doctor's office."

"Of course. Follow me." Olav stepped out and walked in front of us. He pulled out a keycard from his pocket and slid it through. The heavy door buzzed and he opened it. We entered a hallway that smelled heavily of detergents and hospital. I loathed that smell. I always had. Even more since I had started visiting Mads Schou after the accident. It just always reminded me of bad things. Except for the two times in my life when the smell meant giving birth to my two children. But, somehow, I never associated the smell with that...always only with bad things like when Victor had his first big seizure and they kept him for three days examining him and making sure he wasn't epileptic. So many times I had brought him in, wondering if I would ever see him again after they took him out of my arms.

The big door was closed behind us and Olav started walking down the hallway. I looked at the door and felt slightly claustrophobic. I didn't like the thought of being trapped in here and wondered how it made the patients feel. It was, of course, meant to protect the world from these dangerous patients, but I couldn't escape the feeling of being in a prison.

Olav stopped at a door and knocked.

"Come in," a voice said behind it.

Olav opened it and looked at us. "Go ahead," he said with the voice of a gentle giant.

"Thank you," I said and stepped inside.

Morten followed me closely. The woman greeting us on the other side smiled widely and shook Morten's hand. "Doctor R.V. Devulapallianbbhasskar," she said.

"Officer Bredballe," he said.

She scrutinized him while wearing a crooked smile. "Bredballe you say, huh? That's thirty-four, three plus four...you're a seven. You know if you removed that last 'e' in your name, you'd be an eleven. Eleven would suit you much better, Officer. It's a Master number you see. Just a little piece of advice." The doctor winked at him, then turned her head fast to look at me. I had seen her somewhere before, I remembered when looking into her dissecting eyes. Only I had no idea where. She frightened me a little. Especially the way she looked at me.

"And who might you be?" she asked.

I shook her hand. It hurt a little.

"Officer Frost," I lied.

"Frost, huh? Where have I heard that name before? It's a good name for you. Fits you well being a six. You're very caring and nurturing." She pointed at the couch behind me.

"Please, take a seat."

55

APRIL 2014

"So, what can I do for the two of you today?" The doctor asked. She tilted her head slightly and looked at me with a weird smile. Something about her was just eerie.

"We're looking for this girl," Morten said and put a picture of Maya on the table in front of her.

The doctor looked at it, then picked it up. I watched her closely as she studied the picture. My heart skipped a beat. There was something in her expression that convinced me. She knew Maya. She had seen her before.

The doctor shook her head, then put the picture down. "I've never seen her before. May I ask why you're asking me about it?"

"Are you sure?" I asked. "Try looking at it again." I pushed the picture closer to her. The doctor looked again and shook her head even more.

"I...I...really don't think...I mean we have so many people here, could she have been here to visit someone?"

"Do you allow visitors?" I asked.

"If they're family, then yes. Short supervised visits."

"And you think she might have been in here to visit someone?" Morten asked.

"That's not what I said. I said she might have been, but I really don't remember seeing her. It's hard for me to tell, really. Now, was that all?"

"Do you know Mads Schou?" I asked.

The doctor looked startled. "No," she said. She wasn't very good at lying. I could tell she did. "I mean, I heard about what happened to him through the news and everything, but not personally." The doctor looked at her watch, then back at me forcing a smile.

"I have consultations starting here at eight and I need to prepare...was there anything else you wanted from me, officers? I really need to..."

Morten got up. "We won't take anymore of your time, doctor."

It annoyed me that he gave up that easily. I wasn't prepared to let go yet. This was my only clue to finding Maya and I was certain I saw something in her eyes when she saw the picture of her. I wasn't going to let her go that easily.

"Are you sure you don't know where Maya is?" I asked.

"I'm certain...*Officer.*" The doctor paused and looked at me like she knew I wasn't a real officer. That was when I knew I would never get anything out of her.

"Let's go," Morten said, and pulled my elbow.

I rose to my feet and looked at the doctor. I wanted to grab her shoulders and shake her, shake the information out of her. I couldn't bear the fact that she knew something about my daughter's whereabouts and I couldn't force her to tell me. For the first time in my life, I wanted to hurt someone so badly it frightened me. I wanted to scream at her to tell me, to let me know where she had seen Maya, but it was no use.

The doctor reached out her hand. "Let me know if there's anything else I can help you officers with," she said.

I shook her hand, and as I looked at her, I spotted something out of the corner of my eye. What I saw quite startled me.

"I'm afraid you have a rat in your office," I said.

The doctor turned and looked at the big grey rat crawling across her desk. "Ah yes. That's Misty. She's my pet rat."

I felt nauseated. I had always hated rats more than anything. If I had a nightmare, it was always about rats. To me, they were the most disgusting and creepy animals alive. Yet I couldn't stop staring at it. I kept hearing Victor's words in my head.

"Tell her I like pet rats."

Victor never liked rats before. He'd liked many strange things, but never rats. And he never said anything like this without it meaning something.

"Let's go," Morten said.

I stared at the doctor, who was looking at us with a strange almost maniacal smile. I had to really restrain myself from punching that smirk off her face.

56

APRIL 2014

I t was a little reluctantly that I walked out into the hallway following Morten. I wasn't ready to let go of the doctor yet.

"Olav, please help our guests find their way out," the doctor said.

Olav came towards us.

My heart was beating hard in my chest. I had no idea what to do, but I didn't want to leave. I felt so deeply frustrated, I wanted to scream. I turned my head to see if there was something I had missed, but there was nothing but a long hallway painted white. Suddenly, as I looked, a door was opened and another guard walked out of a room, escorting a patient.

"Let's go," Morten said, but for some reason I hesitated. I couldn't take my eyes off of the person exiting the room far down the hallway. I couldn't see her face, but I knew it was her. Something inside of me just knew it. I would recognize my daughter anywhere...no matter the angle...no matter the short blonde hair and different clothes. I just knew.

"Maya?" I yelled and started walking down the hallway. The girl didn't react. The guard started walking in the opposite direction from us and the girl followed.

"Maya?" I yelled again and walked faster.

"Stop," the doctor yelled behind me. "That is a very dangerous patient.

She killed someone just a few days ago. You can't get close to her. She is highly erratic. Olav, you must stop her."

"Emma, stop it. It's not her," Morten said.

But I kept walking...determined steps across the linoleum floor. "Maya?"

I was running. I could hear turmoil behind me and people running after me. I didn't care. I didn't stop. The girl in front of me didn't react. I called again and again, but still she didn't stop. I ran as fast as I could and soon caught up with them. I grabbed her shoulder and turned her to see her face. Then I gasped.

"Maya? Maya, sweetie? It's you. It's really you!"

Tears rolled across my cheeks as I first hugged her, then held her face between my hands while looking into her beautiful eyes. "Oh my God, Maya. I've been so scared."

But Maya didn't react to anything I said. She looked so pale. What was wrong with her?

"Do you know this woman Zelllena?" the guard asked her.

Maya hardly looked at me. She shook her head. "No."

"I'm going to have to ask you to step back," the guard said.

"Zelllena? What is going on here? Maya? Don't you recognize me? I'm your mother."

"I'm sorry Mrs.," the guard said. "I'm going to have to ask you to leave this girl alone."

Olav was behind me now and grabbed my arm. "I'm gonna need you to come with me, Mrs.," he said.

I tried to fight his grip, but he was too strong. "But...but...Maya? But I'm her mother."

"She clearly doesn't know you," the doctor said, approaching us. "I'm sorry, Vivian," she said to the guard. "This woman is very confused. Psychotic after the loss of her daughter. She sees her face everywhere. I'm sorry it had to happen here. Just take Zelllena to her physical therapy. I'll take it from here. Thank you."

"NO!" I screamed while Olav grabbed both my arms and started to drag me out. "That's my daughter! What have you done to her?!"

"Now stop it," Morten said. "This girl is Maya Frost. I know her just as well and I tell you, it's her."

"I'm sorry, Officer," the doctor said. "The girl's name is Zelllena Wold. She was admitted here because she is a danger to herself and others. She was admitted by her parents. If you have issues with her or anyone else in here, you have to take it up with the hospital management. Now I have to ask you to leave."

I watched in shock as the guard took my Maya through a door and she disappeared once again out of my life.

"No!" I pleaded. "Please don't do this. Please don't throw us out of here. I will do anything. I just want to talk to my daughter."

"I'm sorry. I can't help you with that, since this is not your daughter," the doctor said and signaled Olav and another guy. "You're just very delusional because of your loss. It's only natural, but you really should consider getting some help. Now get the two of them out of here before I lose my patience. This is a medical institution not a Kindergarten. I have patients to attend to. Good day, Mrs. Frost."

57

APRIL 2014

I was on the verge of panic when Morten helped me get into the car. I kept yelling and kicking everything. I simply refused to believe that my daughter was right in there and I couldn't do anything about it.

"You're a police officer, Morten. Can't you stop them?" I asked angrily when we drove off. "Can't you go in there with your badge and tell them to give me my daughter?"

He sighed deeply. "I can't, Emma. I have no right to. I'm not even on Maya's case. It's not my district, I'm actually on vacation and I have no authority here. She knows it. And she's right. I need a warrant if I want to force my way in there. Otherwise, I need to go to the hospital management. So I believe that's what we need to do. I'll contact Officer Hansen and try to explain the situation to him. He's the only one who can help us get access to the place."

"And that's going to take what? A week? I can't wait that long, Morten. They'll just move her to some other place. They know we're on to them. What the hell did they do to her? Why couldn't she recognize me?" I burst into tears. Morten put his arm around me. "You should have seen her, Morten. Her eyes...they were completely dead. She stared at me like she had never seen me before. Me! Her mother! I can't believe it."

"I know," Morten said. "It's so surreal. But the important thing right now is to remain calm. At least now we know where she is."

He turned down the road and I watched in the mirror how the hospital disappeared in the background. It broke my heart having to leave my daughter there without knowing if I would ever see her again. It was brutal.

My hands were still shaking as we drove through town. I had never felt so helpless. It was the worst feeling in the world.

"I bet she was the one who pushed Mads," I said. "I mean, she must have been, right? She must have been the one who ran after him and pushed him in front of Maya's car. Then she must have taken Maya and driven off with her. That's the only explanation I can come up with."

Morten parked the car in front of the newspaper's office.

"What are we doing here?" I asked. "I thought we were going to the police station?"

"I'm going," he said. "You stay here with Rebekka and Sune."

"No. I want to go with you. I want to explain everything to Officer Hansen."

Morten put his hand on my shoulder. I hated when he did that. It made me feel like a child.

"You're too upset. You'll come off as a hysterical mother and he won't listen to a word you're saying. Let me talk to him. Officer to Officer."

"But..."

"Trust me on this, Emma. I know how he works. I know how to handle him. I deal with guys like him every day, remember?"

I calmed down. He was right. I was way too agitated and would only ruin everything. "Alright then. I trust you. But tell him you saw her too. You saw her face and had no doubt it was Maya. If it's only me, then he'll think I was just being delusional. And hurry up. If that doctor moves her, then we'll lose her again."

The very thought made my heart jump. This was so tough. Having to wait like this. It was unbearable.

"Meanwhile, I'll explain everything to Rebekka and Sune," I said. "Maybe they can help us somehow. They know everybody in this town."

"I believe more in my way," Morten said. "But it's worth a shot."

I opened the door and got out. I stuck my face inside to say goodbye.

"Just promise me one thing," Morten said.

"Yes?"

"Don't do anything irrational. It's very important. You risk ruining everything. You hear me?"

I smiled and nodded. "I won't," I lied, then slammed the door and ran up the stairs.

58

APRIL 2014

"You'll never guess what we've found out," Rebekka said when I stormed inside the office.

"Wow, what happened to you?" Sune asked when he looked up from his screen. "You look like you just fell from the moon."

"I found Maya," I said. The words felt so strange in my mouth after so many days of searching frantically for her, and so empty, since there was no happiness following them.

Rebekka got up from her chair and walked towards me. "You found her? That's wonderful news!"

I shrugged and swallowed my tears. "It is and it isn't."

"Emma? What's going on? Sit down and let's talk."

I started crying, but tried hard not to. It didn't work. Sune and Rebekka sat next to me on their small couch in the corner. The table in front of me was stacked with newspapers. Sara even took off her headphones and came closer. "I'll get you all some coffee," she said.

"Now tell us everything from the beginning," Rebekka said. "Where did you find Maya? How did you find her?"

I took in a deep breath then started talking. I told them about Mads' Morse signal, about the visit to the ward and me seeing her and her not recognizing me. "She's being kept there for some reason under the name Zelllena Wold."

"What a strange name," Sune said.

"Morten has gone to talk to Officer Hansen and have him help us, maybe through the hospital management or getting a warrant to grant us access."

"But all of that takes time," Rebekka said. "And they might move Maya now that they know you know she's there."

"That's exactly what I tried to tell Morten," I said and sniffled. "But he insists on doing this the right way. You know how he likes to play by the rules."

Sara brought us coffee and carrot cake, then handed me a tissue. I wiped my eyes, then grabbed a piece and took a bite.

"We need to do something," Rebekka said and looked at Sune for answers.

"I'll do some research," Sune said and got up from the couch. He went to sit behind his computer and I heard his fingers dance rapidly across the keyboard. I felt so blessed to have friends like these two in a moment like this.

"What was it you guys found out?" I asked. "You said you found something important?"

Rebekka looked at me. "Ah that. Yes, well it's not as important as your discovery, but I think it is interesting. It's about Signe Schou. I did some digging, well Sune did some and tried to figure out where they went on their honeymoon. We found their credit card information...I know, naughty us for breaking the law."

"Morten isn't here," I said.

"True. What he doesn't know won't hurt him. But anyway. Apparently they went to Egypt at first, but then suddenly bought tickets to Turkey where they stayed only for a little more than a week, then they went to Monaco."

"So they travelled around a little. That's not so strange?" I asked.

"No. But there's more. According to their bank statement, they lost a lot of money at a casino and after that the card was blocked. Sune couldn't trace them anymore, but I found an article in a local paper about two foreigners attacking a family in their home with the intention of stealing money from them, but it ended up with the murder of the wife. There was a picture of one of the arrested. A girl."

"Signe? She was arrested for murder?" I was baffled.

"Apparently, yes. Mads was never found."

"But we know they came back home? How did she go from a prison in Monaco to her mother's basement in Karrebaeksminde?"

"Sune found a way into the police's database down there and found the initial report taken when Signe was arrested, but it also states she was released a week later. She was picked up by a Mrs. Schou. Apparently, all charges were suddenly dropped."

"Mads' mother?" I asked. "Could she have paid them to drop the charges?"

Rebekka shook her head. "She might have paid them, but there was another reason why the charges were dropped. Am I right, Sune?" she asked.

He nodded. "She didn't do it."

"She didn't?"

"No. Apparently, the father in the house they attacked admitted two days later that he did it. He just used the burglary to cover it up. It was the perfect cover. In his statement, he said that the kids entering his home were heavily drugged. No one would believe a word they said. So he took the chance."

"But why? Why did he want to kill the mother?"

"Money. He wanted to get her life insurance. He was indebted...from gambling, like so many others. He told the children he would chop their heads off as well if they ever told he did it. But the oldest daughter broke down during her interrogation and told them everything. Later, the dad admitted the crime. He chopped her head off with an axe and blamed it all on Signe and Mads. The strangest part is that Signe never denied doing it. If you read her statement, all she could talk about was blood. They stated that she kept saying she saw blood everywhere. I guess they figured that was about as good as a confession."

"Maybe she thought she did it?" I asked.

"What do you mean?"

"I mean, she might have been so drugged that she had no idea what was reality and what was in her head."

Rebekka nodded pensively. "It's plausible."

"They were friendly," I suddenly said.

"Who was?"

"Mads and Signe. On Facebook. They wrote something on each other's walls, remember?"

"YNWA," Rebekka said.

"You wouldn't write that if you were angry at each other, would you?"

"Probably not."

I looked at Rebekka. "But I don't know what to make of it."

"Well actually, there was another thing we found," Rebekka said. "Sune found a message from Signe to him on Facebook. She told him to come to the party...that she needed to see him...that it was important. She had something important to say. She pleaded with him to come, but he told her he didn't want to see her. That's probably why she knocked her mother out and escaped from the basement. She went to see him. Maybe she hoped he would show up anyway?"

"But she never showed up," Rebekka said.

"Instead, this strange doctor tried to attack him. Maybe she took Signe as well?"

"But all that doesn't help Maya," Rebekka said.

"It might in the end. So what we need now is a connection between Dr. R.V. Devulapallianbbhasskar and Mads Schou."

"Is that really her name?" Rebekka asked with a grin. "That's ridiculous."

"I know. I think it's a numerology thing. She seems to be into stuff like that. Crystals and numbers. She kept talking to us about our numbers...it's a whole numbers deal, I don't think I understand it anyway. But I'm certain she's the one who attacked him and followed him into the street, then pushed him in front of the car. She seems crazy enough to do it. But why was she after him?"

"That's a good question."

"You might want to hear this," Sune interrupted us.

We both looked at him.

"Ward Q currently has three patients that don't exist."

"What do you mean?" I asked.

"I can't find their names anywhere else, yet they're all admitted to psych Ward Q. I can't even find them in the National Register. They don't exist. One of them is Zelllena Wold."

"Maya," I said.

"Then who are the two others?" Rebekka asked. "Could one of them be Signe Schou?"

"Sascha," I said. "Sascha DuBois. Yes, that's it. Now I remember where I've seen the doctor's face before. On the stairs when walking down after visiting Sascha DuBois the last time. She disappeared after that. She never made it to the police station. The coffee cups were still on the counter. The doctor must have come right when we left. Oh my God, I saw her there. She even said hello to us. Who the hell is this woman?"

"I'm on it," Sune said and started tapping on the keyboard.

I sunk my teeth into yet another piece of cake, feeling anxious and uncomfortable at the thought of this woman having my daughter in her care. It was truly scary.

59

APRIL 2014

It didn't take Sune long to find a lot of background on the dear doctor with the insane name R.V. Devulapallianbbhasskar. I had barely eaten the rest of my cake and washed it down with coffee before he started talking.

"It took a little longer because she's changed her name so many times it's ridiculous," he said. "But from what I could find on her, she became a psychiatrist in 2001 and worked several places until 2006 when she was made Chief of Naestved Institution of Mental Health. But that's not the interesting part. It's what happened to her many years ago. In 1989, when she was only seventeen, she was arrested and convicted of the murder of her own father."

Rebekka looked at me, then at Sune again. "She was what?"

"Her father was found stabbed in their home. Elsebeth Berg, which her name was back then, denied everything, even though they found her fingerprints on the knife. She was evaluated, but found to be mentally fit for a trial. Because of the gruesomeness to the murder and since she was one month from turning eighteen, it was decided to try her as an adult...to set an example, they said. The judge convicted her and sentenced her to twelve years in a secure prison for adults."

"Wow, that was tough," I said. "At seventeen, you said?"

Rebekka looked pensive. "Wasn't there a case once about a seventeen year old who was wrongly put in a prison with adults, then it turned out she was actually innocent?"

"Exactly," Sune said. "Elsebeth spent three years in prison before the mother was arrested for stabbing her new husband. She admitted to having framed her daughter back then, because she thought she would get a lighter punishment, given her age."

"Oh my God," Rebekka said. "I remember reading about this case. It was awful. This poor girl was abused so terribly in prison by the guards and was in an isolation cell for almost six months at one point. The prison warden was fired after it came out that the girl had been badly beaten and sexually assaulted by some of the guards. It was an awful case. It made them completely stop trying teenagers as adults again. She received a huge compensation, as I recall."

"Two million kroner, yes." Sune said.

"And now she's a doctor taking care of our mentally ill patients," I said. "Wow. I think I need to call Morten and tell him this."

I reached for my phone and, as I did, it started to ring. It startled me.

"Hello, Emma Frost? It's Dr. Faaborg here, darling. I'm calling with more great news for you and your daughter."

"What is it?"

"Mads Schou is awake. It's the strangest thing. Apparently, his machines stopped working last night; we still don't know how they got turned off, but it woke him from his coma. This morning, when the nurse came to check on him, he was sitting up looking at her. Then he jumped out of bed and grabbed her and started dancing with her. Can you believe it?"

I was stunned. I had seen the man just last night and he didn't look like anyone who was going to wake up ever. "No, doctor. I really can't. That is truly amazing news."

"Apparently, he was able to hear everything while he was in the coma. He wants to see you. He's tired and a little confused, but keeps asking for the woman whose daughter drove the car. Is it possible for you to come to the hospital?"

I felt confused as well. I really didn't feel like I had the time right now, but the thought of having a reason to go to the hospital where Maya was being kept intrigued me strongly.

60

APRIL 2014

R ebekka and Sune came with me in the car. Rebekka wanted to interview Mads and write about him waking up for the paper. Sune brought his camera. When leaving Karrebaeksminde and heading for the main road towards Naestved, I felt terrible. All those horrible things Sune had read about that doctor made me anxious. An experience like the one she had been through had to make her highly unstable and erratic. I had no idea what she might do to my daughter...and I feared the worst. I couldn't just let time pass and wait for Morten and the police to act, now could I? While that woman did God only knew what to my daughter? How could I? What mother could do that?

I took a turn and accelerated past the town sign.

"Emma, you're not allowed to drive faster than fifty kilometers an hour here," Rebekka said.

I didn't react. I sped past the small houses, zigzagged between the cars and finally arrived at the hospital where I parked in the parking lot in front of the main building. I stopped the engine and stared at the hospital in front of me. I couldn't believe all the times I had been in there to visit Mads Schou and she had been here all the time. Right in the building behind this one. So close and yet I had no idea. It killed me.

"Okay, let's get inside," Rebekka said and got out of the car.

I grabbed my purse. I could hear the blood rushing through my veins.

"Emma, are you alright?" Rebekka asked when I slammed the door to the car. "I know this must be hard for you."

I stopped and stared at the building in front of me. There was no way I could walk in there like I didn't know my daughter was being held captive so close to me.

"There's no way," I mumbled.

"What was that?" Rebekka asked.

"Nothing," I said. "I just...um I think I forgot my phone in the car. Just go on inside. I'll be right there."

"We'll wait here for you," Rebekka said.

"Okay," I said and turned around and walked back to the car. "There's no way, there's no way," I mumbled all the way back, opened the door and got in. I sat in the car seat and pretended to be looking for the phone that I knew was in my purse. I bent my head underneath the dashboard and put the key in the ignition, then turned it, shut the door and before Rebekka and Sune realized what was going on, I hit the gas pedal and accelerated out of the parking lot towards the building with the big Q on a sign outside of it.

I saw Rebekka's face; she was screaming at me, but I heard no sound as I drove past them and accelerated towards the entrance of the building. Seconds later, I bent down as the car slammed through the glass doors and blasted right into the entrance, past the startled lady at the information desk, and directly through the secured double doors Olav had needed a card to get through.

Then it stopped. The car was smashed, smoke was everywhere, but to my relief I saw the car had managed to drive through the doors and reveal the white hallway with the many doors in front of me. There was yelling and screaming behind me and guards trying to reach me, but they couldn't because my car blocked the way. I jumped out through the broken windshield and into the hallway where I fell onto some glass and cut my hand. But I didn't care. My head was hurting from the blow I had received when banging through the doors, but I didn't care about that either. The lady guard from earlier came out of a room and looked at me.

"Vivian," I said, as I reached into my purse and pulled out some mace I always carried in case of an assault. After what had happened to me over the last couple of years, I was done taking chances.

I held the mace up towards her. "Where is she? Vivian, tell me where my daughter is!"

Vivian whimpered, then lifted her hand and pointed. "Right in there," she said.

"Please unlock the door for me."

"But...But I'm not allowed to..."

I moved the mace threateningly towards her. Vivian whimpered again, then put the key in the door and turned it.

"Thank you, Vivian. Now scram! Get the hell out of here. I'm taking my daughter home!"

61

APRIL 2014

I stormed inside the room with the number fifty-seven on the door, holding the mace up in front of me in case more security guards appeared. Then I lowered it again. The sight in front of me made me cry instantly. Days of frustration and worry suddenly rose inside of me and had to get out.

Maya was sitting on the bed staring directly at me. Her eyes were empty and there was no reaction at all when she saw me. I approached her carefully, so I wouldn't frighten her.

"Maya?"

She looked confused. Her eyes were flickering back and forth like she was trying to remember something, but couldn't. I walked to her and kneeled in front of her. I looked up into her eyes.

"Maya? Sweetie?"

Maya still didn't recognize me. I couldn't stop crying. Seeing her like this, all empty, all expressionless was so brutal.

"What did they do to you? Sweetie?"

She still didn't say anything. I cried and pulled her close to me. I hugged her for a long time. She tried to hug me back.

"I'm sorry," she finally whispered. "I'm so sorry. But I don't know who you are. I really don't."

She might as well have punched me in the stomach. She knocked all the air out of me. I had to restrain myself from bursting into tears. Instead, I held her tightly in my arms.

"I'm really sorry," she said again. "I don't know any Maya."

I stroked her hair and tried to hide my sadness. "It's okay, sweetie," I said and held her even tighter.

There were a lot of voices in the hallway now. People were yelling, steps were approaching. I looked at the window under the ceiling. It was barred. There was no way of escaping out of it. I held Maya closer to me as someone pulled the handle and tried to open the door.

"A key someone yelled. We need a key down here."

Maya had started crying and I held her close to me as I heard the key being inserted in the lock and turned. "I'm never letting go of you again, sweetie. Never. It doesn't matter that you don't know I'm your mother. I'll hold on to you. They'll have to take the both of us."

Tears were running down my cheeks as the door was opened and voices entered the room.

"There she is."

I opened my eyes and turned my head. I knew that voice.

"Morten?"

Morten stormed towards us.

"Emma! Maya!" he said.

"Morten! You came!"

Morten kneeled next to me. "I told you we would take care of it," he said. "But you smashing into the building with your car kind of made the process go faster. As soon as the alarm sounded and we were told that a car had driven through a building at the hospital, I knew it could only be you. But it gave us a legit reason for coming in here."

"So for once it paid off to be irrational, huh?"

"Well I don't like to admit it, but I guess it did. Now let's get Maya and you out of here."

I wasn't happy to, but I finally let go of Maya and Morten took her in his arms. Seeing him walk with her like that made me love him more than ever.

62

APRIL 2014

I took Maya to see doctor Faaborg at the main building and told him what had happened. I'm not sure he fully believed me, but he was still so smitten with me that I think he would have done anything for me at that point. He said he would take her in for observation. Meanwhile, Morten hurried back to the ward to help look for Dr. R.V. Devulapallianbbhasskar and arrest her.

Maya fell asleep while I held her hand and then the doctor came in.

"Mads Schou is here," he said. "Now that your daughter is sleeping, maybe you'll have a few minutes to talk to him?"

"I...I can't leave Maya," I said.

"It's okay. I'll come in here," a voice said. Mads Schou entered and smiled at me.

It was strange. I had spent so many hours in his company, but never heard his voice or seen his eyes. I noticed he was very handsome as he came inside the room. You certainly couldn't tell that he had just been in a coma.

"Emma Frost?" he said.

"Yes," I said and wiped make-up away from underneath my eyes.

He grabbed my hand between both of his and shook it, then pulled me close to give me a hug. "Thank you," he said choking. "Thank you so much."

"You're welcome," I answered, quite taken by a surprise by his grateful-ness. I hadn't really done anything had I?

"You saw me when no one else did. I heard you tell the doctor that you had seen me move my finger. You have no idea what that meant to me."

I blushed. "Well, no problem, I guess."

"I heard you say you were sorry for what your daughter did, but I wanted to tell you that I knew all along that she didn't do anything."

"I know," I said. "I know now that you were pushed by that woman, Dr. R.V. Devulapallianbbhasskar."

"How did you know her?" Rebekka asked. "If you don't mind me asking."

"I know your voice," Mads said.

"I interviewed your mother and I visited you with Emma once," she said.

"Lise Lindvig leather boots," he said and looked at her feet. "I remember the sound."

"Wow," she said. "A connoisseur."

"My wife used to have the same pair. Every time you entered I thought you might be her. You asked how I knew the doctor. Well, my mother sent me to see her. After I came home from my honeymoon..."

"We know what happened, well most of it," Rebekka said. "Signe was arrested and falsely accused of murder in Monaco?"

Mads looked at her like he didn't understand. "Falsely? What do you mean by falsely?"

"It wasn't her," I said. "The father admitted to having done it. He killed her, not Signe."

Mads touched his forehead. "You mean to say she didn't do it? But I was certain...I was there..."

"You mean to say you honestly thought she killed that woman?" Rebekka asked.

"Well, yes," he said. "I couldn't remember seeing her do it, but I remember the head and the blood. There was so much blood. I ran into the street...you mean to say she didn't do it? I was tormented by it for months afterwards. That was why my mother sent me to see Dr. R.V. Devulapallianbbhasskar. Despite the strange name, she is known in medical circles as a very good doctor, the best really, and my mother knew her. My mother believed she could help me get rid of all the nightmares and the depression. When it was at its worst, I could hardly get out of bed. But the woman turned out to be a total wacko. I had consultations with her three times a week and, at first, she was really good for me. She really helped me. It took me more than a year, but I opened up and began to tell her things and she listened and never condemned me. She told me she couldn't go to the police because of her vow of confidentiality. So I told her everything. And little by little I started to remember some things and details. But I was still tormented by nightmares. I was constantly afraid that my past would catch up with me. Then she told me she had this program that she wanted me enrolled in...a rehabilitation program for people who had been in trouble with the law and didn't want to go to jail. She told me she had helped many like me. She could change my life. How did she put it again? Oh yes. It was *easy as one, two, three*. She used that phrase a lot, along with all her numerology. By that time, it had started to scare me a little. She had started to ramble on and I didn't trust her much; I was beginning to realize she wasn't sane and it seemed to be getting worse. She showed me around in the ward and told me she could help me if I wanted to. She could give me a new life. She could stop the nightmares and torment by making me forget everything that happened. She could give me a new life, a fresh start, but it meant I had to give up everything, give up everyone I loved. I wasn't ready to do that, so I kindly refused her offer. That was when she went completely mad. She came to my house at night and threatened me with a gun to my head and told me I had to enroll—that it was the only way for me to move on and not end up being abused in prison. I managed to overpower her and get the gun from her and chase her out of the house, but she kept yelling that she would get me sooner or later—she would get me. I didn't believe her until she showed up at the party and tried to inject me with something in the darkness. I ran from her, but she caught up with me."

"And pushed you in front of the car," I said. "In front of Maya who saw Dr. R.V. Devulapallianbbhasskar once she got out of the car and then she attacked Maya instead and took her and put her in her so-called program. Wow."

"But before that, she took Signe as well on her way to the theater to meet me," Mads said. "Dr. R.V. Devulapallianbbhasskar came to my bed last night and told me everything. Right before she shut off my monitors. I never told the doctor here because I was afraid he wouldn't believe me. Dr. R.V. Devulapallianbbhasskar told me last night that she was the one who invited all of us through Facebook. She believed it would make Signe show up...and me as well. Then it was her plan to take the both of us."

"And she was right. You did both decide to go. Why did you decide to go to the party?" Rebekka asked.

"Signe wrote to me and told me she had something important to tell me. To be honest, I wasn't happy about seeing her again not after...well, what I thought had happened in Monaco. I was scared of her, but she was very insistent and I thought I'd give her another shot. I wonder now if she might have remembered that she didn't do it...if that was what she wanted to tell me. My doctor told me the drugs had affected my memory and caused the amnesia, but that I would probably regain my memory slowly. Maybe she got her memory back and wanted to tell me. But I was afraid she would do something terrible again. I decided to take the chance. I wrote something on her wall on Facebook to let her know I was coming."

"YNWA?" I asked.

Mads looked at me startled. "Yes. How did you know?"

"Long story."

Mads looked sad. He shrugged. "How many times have I regretted going to that ridiculous party the last few days? But I guess I wanted to see her. I did, after all, love her once...I think I still do."

I looked at Maya who looked so small and fragile in the big hospital bed that had swallowed her up.

"The drugs made you forget, huh?" My eyes met Dr. Faaborg's who seemed to understand where I was going. "Could you maybe find out what kind of drugs they gave the patients at Ward Q?"

"I'm right on it," he said.

63

APRIL 2014

I didn't leave Maya's side for two entire days. I sat in her hospital room and held her hand when she let me while the doctors examined her and ran a million tests. I couldn't count on one hand the amount of blood tests and brain scans she had gone through. Meanwhile, she remained completely unaware of who I was and who she had been. It was truly devastating.

On the third day, Doctor Faaborg came into the room and pulled me outside to talk to me. We sat down in some chairs right outside her room so I could still keep an eye on the door. They were still looking for Doctor R.V. Devulapallianbbhasskar, but she seemed to have completely vanished. Morten had joined the local police task force to help hunt her down, but I was still terrified that she would come back to hurt Maya.

"I'm afraid Maya suffers from amnesia," Dr. Faaborg said. "I believe it is what we refer to as a *drug-induced amnesia*. I have gone through the files of the Ward she was in and apparently those patients were part of a research project, financed by the pharmaceutical company Lundbit. They were experimenting with drug-induced amnesia as a treatment for psychiatric disorders, such as post-traumatic stress disorder and memory related disorders, such as dementia and Alzheimer's disease. I read a lot about it. By understanding the ways in which amnesia-inducing drugs interact with the brain, researchers hope to better understand the ways in which neurotransmitters aid in the formation of memory. By stimulating, rather than depressing, these neurotransmitters, memory may improve."

"So you're telling me they drugged my daughter as part of an experiment? They made her forget everything?"

"Basically, yes. Amnesia can be partial or whole. I'm afraid hers is whole. She doesn't remember anything. Not even her real name. The drug is currently being used on many of the other patients in the ward with great success. No one in the ward had any suspicion that she was using it on patients that were perfectly healthy."

"I don't understand how a drug like that can help a patient with any disorder like post-traumatic stress. I thought the point of therapy was to make people remember things and work through them?"

Doctor Faaborg nodded. "Yes. But in the process of remembering, the memory needs to be restored in the brain. By introducing an amnesia-inducing drug during this process, the memory can be disrupted. While the memory remains intact, the emotional reaction is dampened, making the memory less overwhelming for the patient. Researchers believe this drug will help patients with post-traumatic stress disorder be able to better process the trauma without reliving the trauma emotionally."

It made sense, I thought. But the thought was horrifying.

"So whole amnesia, huh? She doesn't remember anything at all?" I asked, feeling the tears once again press in on my throat. I wanted to kill that doctor Dr. R.V. Devulapallianbbhasskar for doing this to my daughter. It was so heartbreaking to have to look into her eyes and see the confusion in her...see how sad it made her that she knew I was her mother, since I had told her numerous times, but she couldn't remember me. It killed me.

"I'm afraid not," the doctor said. "Well, you've been there when we've run the tests. You've seen it. She doesn't remember anything from her childhood."

I swallowed a lump in my throat to prevent myself from bursting into tears. I couldn't believe this. It was like a horrendous nightmare. I mean, I was thrilled to have found my daughter and I was so happy to know that she hadn't killed someone in a hit-and-run and that the charges against her were minimized to a fine for driving without a driver's license. I had her back, but still I didn't. This wasn't the Maya I had known and loved. It was her body, yes, but she was nowhere in there. She wasn't herself at all...and I missed her. I missed my strong beautiful caring and very stubborn daughter so badly. I missed holding her in my arms and feeling her hug me back. I missed looking into her eyes and seeing her, seeing all the life all the strength and power she possessed. Now there was nothing. Not even spite.

"But...But...What do I do? How long is it going to last?" My voice was breaking.

Doctor Faaborg put a hand on my shoulder. "There isn't much more we can do for her right now. She is healthy. You take her home, bring her into familiar surroundings with people she loves, then you talk to her. You show her pictures of her childhood and tell her stories that you know she would remember otherwise."

"Will she get her memory back? Ever?" I said, half-choked.

The doctor paused. I didn't like that. "I don't know, Emma darling, I'd like to believe she will. I think we should treat her like any other amnesia patient, but she has been given a very high dose of this drug for days and I have no idea how her brain is going to react to that. I have no experience with patients coming out of a drug-induced amnesia. But remember that she is perfectly capable of making new memories and learning new information."

"So we can start all over, huh? Is that what you're saying? But I don't want to start all over with her. I want her to be herself. I want her to remember me and how much I love her. I want her to remember how much she loves her little brother and how mad I make her, how annoying I can be. I want her to yell at me and roll her eyes at me like she used to. I want her back, Doctor."

"I know. And you might get that. But you have to give her time. Lots of time. And therapy. I'll give you some numbers of physicians in your area you can contact to get the help you need." Doctor Faaborg exhaled. "I wish I could give you better news. I really do. I'm sorry. Good luck with everything and don't be a stranger. Call and let me know how she's doing alright?"

I sniffled and nodded. "Okay. Thank you so much. You've been a great help."

"I'm still shocked that this could have happened in my hospital. I'm so sorry it had to hurt you in this way. I can't believe a colleague of mine could do anything like this. It's truly shocking. Just shows you that you never really know anyone."

I said goodbye to the doctor and went back to Maya, who was sitting up in the bed. She looked at me and tried to smile. I hated that puzzled look in her eyes when she looked at me. It was like she didn't really trust me or trust that I was really her mother.

I forced a smile back. "Great news, sweetie. I can take you home with me now."

I could tell it frightened her. She had no idea where home was or what it looked like.

"I'm sure your brother is going to be thrilled to see you again. He has missed you so much."

Maya looked pensive. "Victor, right?" she asked.

A tear escaped the corner of my eye. I wiped it away before she saw it and nodded. "Yes, yes. That's his name."

I started packing her strange clothes that she had worn at the Ward into a plastic bag, then threw it in the garbage bin. Morten had brought her some of my clothes from the hotel room to wear and I handed them to her so she could get out of the hospital gown. The pants were too big in the waist and the sweater was too long, but she looked adorable. She had lost a lot of weight, I realized. At least that was something I knew I could help correct.

She jumped down from the bed and I reached out my hand to help her. She looked at it for a little while, then at me. I smiled.

"Let's go, sweetie. Let's go home."

Maya nodded, then smiled back. She put her hand in mine. "Yes, Mom. Let's go home."

We walked out of the room and into the hospital hallway hand in hand when someone suddenly yelled behind us. I turned and saw Rebekka and Sune running down the hallway.

"Stooop!" Rebekka yelled. She was holding a box of chocolates in her hand.

I turned to face her with a smile.

Rebekka hugged first me, then Maya. "I'm so glad we made it here before you left!" She handed Maya the chocolates. "These are for you, sweetheart. Make sure you take good care of your mother. She needs you, okay? Make great new memories together."

"I'll try," Maya said a little shy.

Sune hugged her while Rebekka approached me and hugged me again.

"Thank you so much for all your help," I said. "I wouldn't have found her without you. I'm truly grateful for that."

"Well, I don't know about not doing it yourself. You were pretty efficient with that car when you ran it into the building. I don't think anyone but you could have come up with that."

I chuckled. I thought for a second about my talk with the police when they had been here the day before and talked to me about me driving into the building. There weren't going to be any charges, but the hospital was asking for compensation, they said. I figured I didn't owe them anything because of what they did to my daughter and told the police that I would ask for compensation as well. That had shut the Officer up. Now I was just waiting to find out what the hospital's response was going to be to that.

"Did you hear that Mads and Signe Schou are back together?" Sune asked.

"Really? That's great news," I said, feeling truly happy for them. I thought for a second about Morten and all my worries about losing the passion too early in our relationship. Right now, I needed anything but drama and passion. Morten had told me he was going to stay for a couple of days to help with the case and the search for the doctor and suddenly I missed him. I had rented a car to drive me and Maya back to the island. I couldn't wait to see my parents and Victor again. Not to mention Sophia. I had so much to tell her.

"Well, as you know, the police found her and Sascha DuBois at the ward as well and they have both lost their memories just like Maya did, so apparently Mads has decided to take care of his wife. I did an interview with them this morning for tomorrow's paper. It was really sweet. They're starting all over. They're moving to Berlin, he told me. To get away from everything."

Her memories were all bad, after all. If there was anyone who could benefit from forgetting her past it was probably Signe, I thought to myself.

I looked at Rebekka. I had come to care about her. "Thank you for taking me seriously when I needed it," I said. "When the police wouldn't. I'll never forget that. Stop by if you're ever on Fanoe Island, alright?"

Rebekka looked like she was thinking it over. "You know what? We might do just that one day." She stared at me intensely with a grin. "What are you still doing here? Go on. Go home and take care of your daughter."

EPILOGUE
FOUR WEEKS LATER

S he liked the fresh air hitting her face when standing on the top deck of the ferry. She had counted the steps on the stairs to get up there while they were sailing. Fifty-seven. That was five plus seven equals twelve and one plus two equals three. A three wasn't too shabby, the numerologist thought to herself. She would have preferred a four, but she couldn't get everything.

She looked at the island rising in the horizon. Fanoe. She tasted the word. It was a five. The numerologist had come to like that number. Five meant death.

Misty was crawling across her shoulder, tickling her ear with her long whiskers. The numerologist giggled and moved the rat slightly. Then she ran a hand across her new face. She still hadn't gotten used to the way it felt. The nose was so different, so was the chin and especially the lips.

She had taken off as soon as she had realized Emma Frost and her police boyfriend knew she had the daughter. The numerologist had it all planned out, of course she had. She had seen it in the numbers that same morning and knew she had to leave. She had booked a ticket to South Korea where she had heard they were excellent at making your face completely unrecognizable. In fact, they were so good she had heard that some patients who had the operations in some cases were so transformed that they had trouble getting through passport control on the way home. The numerologist didn't have any trouble though, since she had changed her name and bought herself a brand-new passport in South Korea from a man she had learned was a master in forging. A master he had been, indeed. The man in the passport control at the airport hadn't even blinked when looking at it.

"Yes, Misty. You and me. Doctor Sonnichsen and Misty. We make a great team, don't we?"

She tasted the new name. It fit her well, she thought. It was a three. Three was good. It was more compatible with her birthdate. She shook her head, thinking about that silly name she had left behind. R.V. Devulapallianbbhasskar. Ha! She should have known it would go wrong, with that name. Having an R before a V simply didn't work. Any fool knew that!

The numerologist looked at the rat that had been her companion the last three years. Before that, she had another rat also named Misty. It had been like that ever since her time in the isolation cell in Herstedvester Prison when she had spent six months with no other companionship than a rat that lived inside the mattress she was supposed to sleep on. It had soon become her best friend and she had called it Misty.

"Yes, Misty," she said and petted it. She lifted it up towards her mouth and kissed it, feeling its teeth against her lip. "You and me, we will be together forever. We're family, remember?"

The ferry was getting close to the island now and they were told to get back into their cars. The numerologist looked at the island approaching before she decided to go. On her way down, she met an old man who looked at her with a smile.

"Is it your first time on Fanoe Island?" he asked.

The numerologist chuckled. "Yes. Never been here before."

"Well, welcome," he said. "Business or pleasure?"

"A little bit of both," she said. "I have some unfinished business and it will be my pleasure to put an end to it."

The End

———

Want to know what happens next? Get the 8th installment in the Emma Frost Mystery here: http://www.amazon.com/There's No Place like Home

AFTERWORD

Dear Reader,

Thank you for purchasing *Easy as One Two Three*. I hope you enjoyed it. I want to let you know the story of Mads being able to hear everything while in a coma is taken from a true story that I read recently. I found it very creepy and knew I had to put it in a book.

This was a really fun book for me to write. I loved being able to bring in Rebekka and Sune again and find out how they were doing. I don't think this will be the last we see of them.

To those of my readers who didn't recognize them, then I can tell you that they are the main characters in my other mystery-series, the Rebekka Franck Series. If you haven't already read those books, then you can get them by following the links below.

Don't forget to check out my other books if you haven't already read them. Just follow the links below. And don't forget to leave reviews, if you can.

Thanks for all your support. I have the best readers in the world.

Take care,
   Willow

ABOUT THE AUTHOR

The Queen of Scream aka Willow Rose is a #1 Amazon Best-selling Author and an Amazon ALL-star Author of more than 80 novels. She writes Mystery, Paranormal, Romance, Suspense, Horror, Supernatural thrillers, and Fantasy.

Willow's books are fast-paced, nail-biting page-turners with twists you won't see coming.

Several of her books have reached the Kindle top 20 of ALL books in the US, UK, and Canada.

She has sold more than six million books all over the world.

Willow lives on Florida's Space Coast with her husband and two daughters. When she is not writing or reading, you will find her surfing and watch the dolphins play in the waves of the Atlantic Ocean.

f facebook.com/willowredrose

twitter.com/madamwillowrose

instagram.com/madamewillowrose

Copyright Willow Rose 2017
Published by BUOY MEDIA LLC
All rights reserved.

No part of this book may be reproduced, scanned, or distributed in any
printed or electronic form without permission from the author.

This is a work of fiction. Any resemblance of characters to actual persons,
living or dead is purely coincidental. The Author holds exclusive rights to
this work. Unauthorized duplication is prohibited.

Cover design by Juan Villar Padron,
https://juanjjpadron.wixsite.com/juanpadron

Special thanks to my editor Janell Parque
http://janellparque.blogspot.com/

———

Lightning Source UK Ltd.
Milton Keynes UK
UKHW041935200121
377415UK00013B/636/J